PRAISE FOR P9-CEU-222

A YEAR IN THE LIFE OF A COMPLETE AND TOTAL GENIUS

Winter 2015–2016 Indie Next Pick

Junior Library Guild Selection

2016 Notable Children's Book in the Language Arts
by the Children's Literature Assembly

"[A] humorous coming-of-age novel."

—*Publishers Weekly*

"With lots of warmth, humor, and sly wit, Canadian author Matson introduces readers to one of the funniest characters to ever cross the pages of middle-grade literature. With his story told through a series of emails, journal entries, and memos, Arthur Bean is a unique new voice not soon to be forgotten."

—*Shelf Awareness*

"At once funny, outrageous, thoughtful, and informative, this is a story with something for everyone, and Arthur's is a voice readers won't soon forget."

—*The Manitoba Library Association*

"Fans of Tommy Greenwald's Charlie Joe Jackson series will be drawn to Arthur."

—*Booklist*

"Written entirely in notes, emails, stories, and journal entries, this novel successfully captures the trials and tribulations of junior high school."

—*School Library Journal*

SCENES FROM THE EPIC LIFE OF A TOTAL GENIUS

ALSO BY STACEY MATSON

A Year in the Life of a
Complete and Total Genius

SCENES FROM THE EPIC LIFE OF A TOTAL GENIUS

STACEY MATSON

sourcebooks
jabberwocky

Copyright © 2015 by Stacey Matson
Cover and internal design © 2016 by Sourcebooks, Inc.
Text copyright © 2015 by Stacey Matson
Illustrations by Simon Kwan © 2015 by Scholastic Canada Ltd.
Cover design by Will Riley/Sourcebooks, Inc.
Cover images © malerapaso/Getty, vasabii/Thinkstock

Sourcebooks and the colophon are registered trademarks of Sourcebooks, Inc.

All rights reserved. No part of this book may be reproduced in any form or by
any electronic or mechanical means including information storage and retriev-
al systems—except in the case of brief quotations embodied in critical articles or
reviews—without permission in writing from its publisher, Sourcebooks, Inc.

The characters and events portrayed in this book are fictitious and are used
fictitiously. Any similarity to real persons, living or dead, is purely coincidental
and not intended by the author.

Published by Sourcebooks Jabberwocky, an imprint of Sourcebooks, Inc.
P.O. Box 4410, Naperville, Illinois 60567-4410
(630) 961-3900
Fax: (630) 961-2168
www.sourcebooks.com

Originally published as Scenes from the Epic Life of a Total Genius in 2015 in
Canada by arrangement with Scholastic Canada Ltd.

Library of Congress Cataloging-in-Publication data is on file with the publisher.

Source of Production: Worzalla, Stevens Point, Wisconsin, USA
Date of Production: September 2016
Run Number: 5007435

Printed and bound in the United States of America.
WOZ 10 9 8 7 6 5 4 3 2 1

For Andrew,
my underappreciated, overly teased,
and awesome little brother.

SEPTEMBER

September 3rd

Dear RJ,

Did you miss me? I missed having you around. Camp was crazy, but now I have the skills to make an award-winning documentary that tells all about a boy genius! Ha-ha-ha. Oh, RJ, I bet you missed my sense of humor!

I have so much to tell you, and it's not all that boring stuff like last year. I guess I could call you something else now. I kind of like RJ though. Instead of standing for "Reading Journal," maybe now RJ means "Really Juicy"—as in the gossip I have for you.

This summer was epic! For one thing, I really thought arts camp would suck, but it was pretty cool. I wish I had time to tell you all about it right now, but I'm leaving to go and hang out with my girlfriend.

That's right. I said MY GIRLFRIEND. I told you I have a lot to tell you, but you'll have to wait!

Yours truly,
Arthur Bean

▶▶   ▶▶   ▶▶

Dear Eighth Graders:

Welcome back! I hope you had a restful summer and are ready for another exciting year of English class. I'm pleased to see many of the same faces as last year, and I look forward to helping you grow your skills as writers and critical thinkers.

There are things that we will need to cover as part of the curriculum, but there's some room in the year for us to focus on things that are important to you. Please write a short paragraph on what you want to get out of this class this year. What do you like about English class? What do you dislike? What are your favorite things to talk about? To write? How do you like to learn? Do you prefer to work alone, or do you like working in pairs or groups? How can this classroom be your ideal space for learning?

Due: September 6

▶▶   ▶▶   ▶▶

Dear Ms. Whitehead,

You'll be pleased to know that I'm a new man this year. That's right. Things have turned around 180 degrees. No more writer's block for me. I'm literally bursting at the seams with ideas and things to write. I don't know if there's enough paper in the world for all the awards I'm going to win for my ideas. I'm not sure how many different genres you have to be good in to win a Nobel Prize, but I'm definitely on my way to mastering the written word.

Something that I would like to do is film related. We should watch a lot of Hollywood movies so that we can write good scripts. I learned a lot about making films this summer, and I would like to write scripts for blockbusters, which requires seeing what great directors do. My girlfriend says that most movies are written by more than one person, so if we work in partners, I want to work with Robbie because we wrote a really good script together this summer, and we're making a movie this year.

If we can't work together, I would like to work alone.

I also think that I would learn more from class if we can have Fridays off, because then I can focus on what we learn the other days and have time to reflect on your teachings. My girlfriend goes to an alternative school where they have very flexible schedules, and I think our school should have those too.

I also think that my desk should be beside the window for me to have the most ideal learning space. I do my best work when I can reflect on nature.

Yours truly,
Arthur Bean

Dear Arthur,

Thank you for your detailed feedback. I will do my best to accommodate everyone's wishes; however, not everyone can sit next to the window. As far as scriptwriting goes, I'm glad to hear that you've taken an interest in a new way of writing! You should consider joining the AV Club, as we won't be doing much scriptwriting and filmmaking in class. I'm pleased to hear that you and Robbie have become friends. I look forward to seeing all your creative work this year.

Ms. Whitehead

⏵⏵   ⏵⏵   ⏵⏵

September 8th

Dear RJ,

Man, having a girlfriend takes up a lot of time. We have these really long text conversations for hours, even though it's really boring. I don't actually have that much to say.

Which reminds me—I have a new phone! Dad gave it to me when I got back from camp. It's nice of him, but it's a piece of crap—no touch screen or anything! At least I can text, but I can't do anything else on it. I want a phone that shoots movies. It would be awesome if it shot movies in 3-D! I could make mini documentaries and go viral. I'll start with videos of Pickles. Everyone loves cat videos—that's what my girlfriend says.

Speaking of my girlfriend, you're probably wondering who she is. Her name is Anila, and I met her at camp this summer. Anila was in the Juniper cabin, and she's in eighth grade too. She lives in Calgary, but she goes to this alternative school where they never have to go to class and they spend their days doing art and making soufflés or something. She's really nice. I mean, she definitely wasn't the coolest girl at camp—there were other girls who were *awesome*—but she's super smart. She's really environmental as well. She even started a compost program for her whole school. When I came home, I tried to compost here. After a week the cupboard under the sink had maggots and flies everywhere and it stank! So my dad threw out the bucket I was using to collect food scraps, and I think he has to call someone to clean it out with industrial-strength bleach. I told him that I didn't think that would be very environmental, but he said he didn't care at all about the environment right now—not very green of him. So now I'm diluting all the soap bottles by adding water to make them last longer.

I haven't told Anila because I want her to think that I'm really environmental as well, so if I brag about it, she'll know that I wasn't environmental *before* camp started. I'll just bring it up in conversation casually the first time she comes over. I can say, "Oh, by the way, you may find that the soap is really watery. That's because I dilute it with water to make it last longer. It's better for the environment."

I invited her for supper next weekend, which means Dad and I will have to make something from scratch and not just frozen food. I asked Nicole for help, and she said that her new boyfriend is a chef, so he's got great recipes. I'm glad she's next door. She's like my adult friend, even though she doesn't act like a real adult most of the time.

Yours truly,
Arthur Bean

▸▸   ▸▸   ▸▸

dude, remmember the thing we were talking about? i have to talk to u about it

Did someone find out? Did you tell someone? ROBBIE!! I knew it was a terrible idea! I told you that already!

chill out artie. its not that big a deal. its just i need u to keep it.

Why? I don't want it anywhere near me!

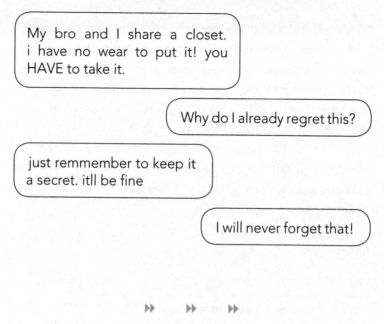

My bro and I share a closet. i have no wear to put it! you HAVE to take it.

Why do I already regret this?

just remmember to keep it a secret. itll be fine

I will never forget that!

From: Kennedy Laurel (imsocutekl@hotmail.com)
To: Arthur Bean (arthuraaronbean@gmail.com)
Sent: September 8, 20:16

Hi Arthur!

I've missed you! Where have you BEEN all my life? LOL!!!! In case you were wondering, Malaysia was good, but SOOO hot LOL! It got kind of boring sometimes, but I don't think you're allowed to complain if you get to go to exotic places LOL! Anyway, I hope you had a good summer! Are you glad to be back at school? I didn't want to go back to school, but I really like getting new clothes and buying pens and paper and school supplies! I know! What a DORK LOL!!!

It's too bad that we're not in the same English class! I have Mrs. Ireland, and I've heard that she's SUPER strict! I guess we'll still see each other at the newspaper meetings, right? Do you have Mr. Everett for science this year?!? He's SUCH a dork, but I still like him! He's like the Perry White of Junior High Newspapers (FYI: I TOTALLY had to google "the editor from *Superman*" to make that joke! I'm SO geeky LOL!) Anyway, I just want to make sure you're still ALIVE! See you tomorrow at the Newspaper Club!

Kennedy ☺

From: Arthur Bean (arthuraaronbean@gmail.com)
To: Kennedy Laurel (imsocutekl@hotmail.com)
Sent: September 8, 22:04

Dear Kennedy,

I missed you too! You should write a travel book or something about Malaysia. I bet you would boost their tourism by one hundred percent!

Anyway, my summer was actually good—way better than last year. Robbie and I were the most popular guys at arts camp (not surprising, ha-ha-ha), and it was actually really cool. We learned all kinds of things about filmmaking, and we're going to make a blockbuster movie. We're going to get everyone in the school to be in it, even just as extras or something. Of course you'll have to be one of the stars! We already have a really good camera. It is super expensive and does amazing things to make your shots look professional. Ms. Whitehead suggested that we join the AV Club, which I guess we'll have to do if we want to use the editing software and stuff. It kind of sucks that we have to join because the kids in the AV Club are annoying. They think they know everything! Plus, Mrs. Ireland is in charge. If she's strict in class, I bet she's the same for AV projects. But I guess we'll do it for our art.

Yours truly,
Arthur Bean

PS: I'm definitely in for the newspaper this year. Mr. Everett said last year that I could have my own opinion column this year!
PPS: Nice work on the *Superman* reference. Even if you had to google it.

From: Kennedy Laurel (imsocutekl@hotmail.com)
To: Arthur Bean (arthuraaronbean@gmail.com)
Sent: September 8, 22:50

Hi Arthur!

So you're going to be a famous movie director! That's AWESOME! I can't wait to hear all about your camp adventures! I've never been to summer camp, but every book and movie about it makes it sound like there's LOADS of adventures and romance LOL! And I'll DEFINITELY be in your movie! I was born to be a star, baby!! LOL! LOL!!!

Kennedy ☺

▶▶   ▶▶   ▶▶

September 9th

Dear RJ,

Well, dinner with Anila and my dad was kind of a bust. My dad seemed to be doing his best mime impression and barely said anything. Anila tried to ask him about yoga, but he didn't have anything to say. And my choice of menu was a little off. It's a good thing we had the salad, because I forgot that Anila is half-vegan, so she barely ate any of the chicken pasta, and she talked about how awful it is how chickens are raised. I didn't realize how terrible chickens have it. I just wish that they didn't taste so good. I'll have to try to be more vegan, I guess. Although I don't know what exactly a vegan is. I think it's a fancy vegetarian.

I had kind of forgotten what Anila was like. I haven't really seen her since coming back from camp. She doesn't think my jokes are hilarious (which, for the record, RJ, they are). She kind of laughs at them, but a lot of the time she pauses a long time before she laughs. I asked her about it once, and she said that she does think I'm funny, but that sometimes she doesn't get it right away because English is her second language—which is weird because her English is perfect. And she talks a lot. She actually talks almost as much as Kennedy, but about different things, like current events. It made me think that I should read the newspaper more.

Know what was the strangest part though? I'm really happy to see Anila and hang out with her, and I like getting texts from her, but I don't really think about her when she's not there. It's almost like I forget that I have a girlfriend. Is that bad?

Yours truly,
Arthur Bean

▸▸   ▸▸   ▸▸

ZOMBIE SCHOOL MOVIE

by Arthur Bean and Robbie Zack

I, Arthur Bean, hereby declare an equal partnership between Robbie Zack and Arthur Bean on the making of the next Hollywood blockbuster movie, where zombie teachers take over a school and it's up to the coolest, most awesome students to destroy them and restore order to a troubled universe. We declare that we will meet every couple of weeks to write and direct our movie, where we both do equal amounts of work and both of us get credit for everything all the time, no matter whose idea it is. I decree that I promise to write down all the important things because Robbie hates doing that, and he will sketch out scenes, or, as we call them in the biz, storyboards.

It is through this official contract that we will create the greatest movie ever created by eighth graders in Canada, equally.

Signed,
Arthur Bean
Robbie Zack

▶▶   ▶▶   ▶▶

Hi, Artie!

Welcome back to the Newspaper Club! With
some of last year's members returning, it
looks like "read" will be the hottest color at
Terry Fox Junior High this year!
   The eighth-and-ninth-grade band is
going to Ontario (OnTerrible is more like
it!—Just kidding! I'm from there!) this year
for MusicFest! To help them get there, they
are doing a silent auction of goods and
services. Mr. Eagleson had some concerns
about not getting enough people and asked if

the newspaper could help out by giving them some free advertising. Would you be able to talk to Mr. Eagleson and find out what kind of prizes they have and what MusicFest is and write something that will get students interested in bidding on their auction? That would be as grand as a piano!

Mr. E

▸▸   ▸▸   ▸▸

From: Kennedy Laurel (imsocutekl@hotmail.com)
To: Arthur Bean (arthuraaronbean@gmail.com)
Sent: September 12, 20:49

Hi Arthur!

A whole bunch of us are going to the mall on Saturday to hang out, like me and Jill and Catie and I think even Robbie and maybe Ben?!? Do you want to come? It's supposed to be SUPER rainy outside! Maybe the mall isn't your thing though LOL! We're probably just going to eat fries and wander around!!

Kennedy ☺

▸▸   ▸▸   ▸▸

From: Anila Bhati (anila.i.bhati@gmail.com)
To: Arthur Bean (arthuraaronbean@gmail.com)
Sent: September 13, 13:06

Dear Arthur,

I know you're at school right now, but I was thinking about you and thought I would write you an email! I have computer lab time right now. I was going to use it to start a letter-writing campaign to my MP, but I couldn't get focused. So, instead of doing my work, I'm writing you an email.

I was thinking about how amazing it is that we met. I mean, the chances are slim that we will ever meet someone who is so in tune with who we are, and to meet at the same camp and be from the same city—it is truly something... Remember that old oak tree at camp? You know, the one where everyone carves their initials, and you can see the people's initials disappear as the tree grows... Some people's initials are probably not even visible anymore. Let's make a promise to not be like those initials and be remembered together forever.

I was looking earlier at articles about the North. Did you hear about the polar bears? They're disappearing too. It's awful, isn't it? I'd love to know what you think... I miss talking to you about this stuff!

I can't wait to see you on Saturday. I hope we are still going to hang out! I miss you!

Love,
Anila

From: Arthur Bean (arthuraaronbean@gmail.com)
To: Anila Bhati (anila.i.bhati@gmail.com)
Sent: September 13, 19:33

Dear Anila,

I'm not really sure if the tree with initials was an oak. I think that it was a different type of tree, like a spruce maybe? Oaks have leaves, and I'm pretty sure that the initial tree has needles. Also, I think you can see all the initials on it.

Anyway, your email is really nice. I can't wait to see you either. I was thinking of going to the mall on Saturday, but I know you hate it, so I can do that before we hang out. It's supposed to rain on Saturday. Also, I've been reading stuff in school about oil spills, and they are really bad for the environment too! We can talk about that if you want to.

Yours truly,
Arthur Bean

From: Anila Bhati (anila.i.bhati@gmail.com)
To: Arthur Bean (arthuraaronbean@gmail.com)
Sent: September 13, 21:09

Dear Arthur,

I prefer to think of the tree as an oak. The symbolism is more powerful. I'll call it poetic license. ☺

You're right. I do hate the mall. There's just so much to buy and there's no need for any of it! I could meet you there though, if you have to go. Then we could go to the park. Or, actually, there's this thing…a few people from school were talking about cleaning up the park nearby. We could do that!

I also read this M. T. Anderson book this week. It was very bleak, and the future is so overwhelmed by advertising and technology that there are Internet feeds literally inside the brains of the characters. Maybe I'll bring it for you to borrow. I think you will appreciate the social message.

Love,
Anila

From: Arthur Bean (arthuraaronbean@gmail.com)
To: Anila Bhati (anila.i.bhati@gmail.com)
Sent: September 14, 8:12

Dear Anila,

Let's not meet at the mall. I can get the stuff I need there later. I don't want you to have to go and be bored.

I've read that book, I think. Is it *Feed*? I liked it. It was really funny the way language was all screwed up.

See you on Saturday.

Yours truly,
Arthur Bean

▶▶   ▶▶   ▶▶

dude too bad u didnt come to the mall. it was fun.

I really wanted to come! What did you guys do?

Hey, I'm just curious, but is Kennedy dating anyone right now? She never said anything. I'm just curious. No reason.

u missed out. kennedys brother was there 4 a bit tho + he's a total turd. how was ur gramma?

Hey, do you want to hang out and plan the movie tomorrow? My dad can drop me off and pick me up.

▶▶   ▶▶   ▶▶

Assignment: Description and Imagery

I've asked you to bring in three objects that each have personal meaning for you. Choose one of these objects and write a short piece about its importance. Make sure that you describe it: What does it look like? What does it feel like? Does it have a taste? A smell? Why is it important?

Due: September 24

⏩ ⏩ ⏩

September 17th

Dear RJ,

Kennedy actually came and sat with me and Robbie at lunch for a bit. I mean, not for the whole lunch, but she sat down at our table and talked to us about the AV Club. She said that Mr. Everett was thinking that she should write a piece for the newspaper about some of the clubs people could join and he wants the AV Club on the list. The thing is, Robbie and I aren't sure that we want a bunch of nerds joining our project. What if they have really terrible ideas? So I told her that we aren't letting people in except by invitation only.

Yours truly,
Arthur Bean

⏩ ⏩ ⏩

The Day the Band Went Silent

by Arthur Bean

This is the end of the concert band at Terry Fox Junior High.
    That is, it could be if they don't get the support and money for their band trip. The senior concert band is in dire need of

some money to help get them to Ontario to compete in this year's MusicFest, a national competition of junior high concert bands that is held every other year in Ottawa, Ontario. Terry Fox Junior High has been invited to compete in this battle of the bands, but they can't go without help from the rest of the school.

Older students will probably remember last year's fund-raising attempt, a time that will forever be referred to as the Culturally Insensitive Christmas Wrapping Paper Debacle. This year Mr. Eagleson is hoping that a silent auction will bring in the money that the band desperately needs.

A *silent* auction, you say? Auctions are typically held with a fast-talking auctioneer. A silent auction requires bidders to write down the bid for their item on a piece of paper. Each bid must be higher than the bid written down before it. On the final day, the last bid on each piece of paper will be the winner. The silent auction will run from October 10 until October 19, when the winners will be announced. The auction will also be open during parent-teacher interviews on the evenings of October 17 and 18.

Mr. Eagleson said that there are some great items up for auction. A list of items can be found on page three. Remember: IF you don't buy something, a piece of the arts will die.

Hiya, Artie!

This is a little extreme, don't you think? Don't get me wrong, buddy, I like the way you make the arts important, but I'm not sure that this is the right tone for a piece where we want people to buy things! I really like the paragraph explaining how a silent auction works, and your sly wink to last year's Christmas paper fund-raiser made me smile. But let's work on this article at lunch and see if we can't strike a different chord for the band! ☺

Cheers!
Mr. E

Dear Mr. Everett,

Remember how last year we talked about how I had such a strong voice in my writing that I would do a great job at having my own column? I just thought this would be a good time to start running that as a regular feature in the newspaper. We have a new generation of news readers, Mr. Everett, and I know they will appreciate my unique perspective. Without it, the news is so boring! If you like, I could focus on one thing, like writing about movies. I'm learning so much about them, and I'm sure people would appreciate an insider's view of filmmaking.

Yours truly,
Arthur Bean

Hi, Artie!

I'm not sure about having your own column, but let's see what you do with a perspective piece! As you know, the annual

Terry Fox Run is coming up. Since its inception, our school has been a benchmark for participation in the run, and I'm really hoping that you can write a piece for the paper. On your mark, get set, go!

Mr. E

⏩   ⏩   ⏩

ZOMBIE SCHOOL

by Arthur Bean and Robbie Zack

September 21 Production Meeting

Notes from today's meeting:
As script director, I feel certain that my idea of having a "ghosts vs. zombies" movie could be the greatest twist ever, because no one will see it coming (HA-HA-HA! Ghosts... See them coming!!). When the students turn out to already be dead but coming back to life as they are killed by zombies, it will be the most epic battle scene of all time. Robbie says it's stupid. I'm writing down my idea because Robbie will realize that I was totally right and that it will be amazing. Then I will show him this paper and it will serve as proof that I was right and he was wrong. (Read it and weep, future Robbie Zack!)

We also decided that our production company will not be called BEAN THERE, DONE ZACK PRODUCTIONS like I wanted, but it will be called MISERABLE WOLVERINE PRODUCTIONS.

▸▸   ▸▸   ▸▸

From: Kennedy Laurel (imsocutekl@hotmail.com)
To: Arthur Bean (arthuraaronbean@gmail.com)
Sent: September 21, 20:31

Hi Arthur!

How's it going? Robbie told me that you guys want to be featured in my newspaper article! That's awesome!!! I can't wait to INTERVIEW you! Don't worry! I'll make you look like the COOLEST film nerds at the school LOL!! I totally want to be in your movie too! The play this year sounds SUPER lame, so you probably won't have a lot of competition getting good actors from the drama department LOL!! ANYWAY, I was thinking we could do the interview tomorrow! I have a family thing in the morning, but we could meet at the mall and do the interview there! I told Mr. E I would have the story done by Thursday, so you BETTER be available!

Kennedy ☺

From: Arthur Bean (arthuraaronbean@gmail.com)
To: Kennedy Laurel (imsocutekl@hotmail.com)
Sent: September 21, 20:55

Dear Kennedy,

Sure, I can meet you whenever you want! Meeting outside school is a great idea. We barely get to talk at school, so that would be awesome.

Yours truly,
Arthur Bean

PS: We "film nerds" actually prefer the term "film geek." It's more inclusive. ☺

▸▸   ▸▸   ▸▸

Hi, Anila. I know we said that we would meet tomorrow, but now I have to work on a project for a class, so I can't make it. Sorry!

I'm disappointed that I won't get to see you, Arthur, but I understand. I hope your project goes well. What's it on? XOXO

My class is working on a study of alternative energy sources... I can't wait to tell you about it. Maybe we could write some letters to companies about switching to different fuel sources! XOXO

How are things otherwise? Did you watch the documentary I told you about? I really think you'll find it interesting, and you'll probably never eat beef again... XOXO

I'll watch it tonight if I can. I have a lot of homework though. Sorry about tomorrow. Good night!

Good night to you too, Arthur Bean! I miss you a lot! XOXO

▶▶   ▶▶   ▶▶

September 22nd

Dear RJ,

Oh, man! There was such a close call today! I was at the mall with Kennedy and Robbie when Anila walked by! She was there BY HERSELF and she walked past the food court. I don't know what she was doing there; she's always talking about how she never goes! Thankfully, she didn't see us. But I was so focused on her not seeing us that I wasn't listening to Kennedy's questions, so I didn't sound as awesome in the interview as I wanted to. Now she'll probably focus on Robbie, and he'll sound like he's in charge of our movie when really it's me.

Know what's weird though? I was so worried that Anila was going to see us, but I was even more nervous that Kennedy would find out about Anila! I don't know why I don't want her to know that I have a girlfriend, but I don't. Anila and Kennedy are two different parts of my life, and I like having them separate. My mom used to say that she never mixed her work friends and her other friends. It's kind of like that, I guess.

Yours truly,
Arthur Bean

▸▸   ▸▸   ▸▸

25

Assignment: My Camp Necklace

by Arthur Bean

My object is my hemp necklace from arts camp this summer. I made it, and I thought jewelry making would be lame, but it wasn't. It's actually really easy to make a hemp necklace. It's basically just tying fancy knots and adding beads. I think my knitting prowess helped me, because it turned out pretty awesome. One of the beads is plain navy blue. I chose it because blue was my mom's favorite color and I knew she would have liked that one best.

One bead is a skull and crossbones because there were only two beads like that and Robbie got them both and gave one to me so that we would both have one. The next one has a spider on it, and I chose it because of my camp counselor, Spider. Spider wasn't his real name. It's his camp name. He was this huge black dude who was over six feet tall. He was just always really cool about everything, and he told me that when his dad died, he was around my age. He didn't make a big deal about it, but he was easy to talk to all the time. I was kind of nervous around him at first, but then at a campfire one night, he brought his guitar out and he was this amazing classical guitarist. Almost everything about him was awesome and kind of surprising actually.

I really like my necklace, because it's softer now after I've worn it every day for a couple of months. I didn't ever need to take it off, because it was waterproof too. Well, not really waterproof, but it didn't get ruined in the water. I wore it for the first few days of school, but a bunch of people made fun of me for wearing jewelry, including Robbie (even though he wore his every day at camp), so I took it off and now I keep it on my bedpost so I get to at least see it every night.

Dear Arthur,

I'm pleased to see the thought you've put into this assignment. You've done a great job here; the accomplished writer in you shines through! I hope that all your assignments this year are of such quality.

Ms. Whitehead

OCTOBER

October 1st

Dear RJ,

Robbie brought the video camera to school on Friday, and I had to carry it in my backpack all day. I guess I could have put it in my locker, but I didn't want it to get stolen. Which is actually pretty funny, considering where it came from.

I probably shouldn't say anything more, at least not in writing. Evidence and all that. But you should know that I am really starting to hate this video camera. Just having it in the apartment makes me feel like the cops could knock on the door any minute now.

Yours truly,
Arthur Bean

▸▸　　▸▸　　▸▸

From: Anila Bhati (anila.i.bhati@gmail.com)
To: Arthur Bean (arthuraaronbean@gmail.com)
Sent: October 1, 17:54

Hi, Arthur!

My mother wanted me to invite you and your father over for Canadian Thanksgiving dinner next Sunday. My mom and my grandmother are going to be making a feast of Indian food, including homemade naan bread that is so light and buttery it makes my mouth water just thinking of it… You and your father wouldn't have to bring anything at all, but my parents would love to see you again and meet your dad. My father really likes movies, so you can talk about that with him. And my mother thinks it's just lovely that you knit. I showed her the coffee-cup sleeve that you knitted for me at camp, and she thinks you should sell them at craft fairs! Have you ever thought about that?
  Anyway, I really do hope you can make it.
  I miss you!

XOXO
Anila

▶▶   ▶▶   ▶▶

October 1st

Dear RJ,

Anila invited me and Dad over for Thanksgiving. Anytime this happens in a book or a movie, it's a big deal, so I guess I should be worried about it. I don't know why though. Maybe our parents will be friends. My dad could use more friends. He goes to yoga still, but other than that, he doesn't really do much. That being said, I'm kind of glad that he hasn't started dating or something, the way Robbie's dad has. That would be the worst. Actually, the worst would be if he started dating a teacher. That happens in movies and novels all the time. Thankfully, I don't think Ms. Whitehead would be his type. At least, I hope she's not his type. I couldn't handle it.

But other than our parents meeting, I don't know why I should worry—except about all that curry in one meal. Anila told me that her mom's cooking is really spicy. I can't eat spicy things without it getting really, really embarrassing.

I wonder what Kennedy is doing for Thanksgiving. I don't think she's got a boyfriend right now. The tables have turned. Now I have a girlfriend and she's single. Maybe this is a parallel universe?? Ha!

Yours truly,
Arthur Bean

▸▸   ▸▸   ▸▸

From: Arthur Bean (arthuraaronbean@gmail.com)
To: Anila Bhati (anila.i.bhati@gmail.com)

Sent: October 2, 9:33

Hi, Anila!

I talked to my dad, and we can come for dinner on Thanksgiving Sunday. It works out really well, because our friend Nicole and her boyfriend invited us over for dinner on Monday night. So it's perfect! Like my dad said, we will get to have curry and turkey and we won't have to do any of the cooking or the dishes!

Yours truly,
Arthur Bean

▶▶   ▶▶   ▶▶

Pounding the Pavement: The Terry Fox Run

by Arthur Bean

I think we can all agree that Terry Fox was a hero. He was strong and brave and an amazing athlete. But I need to take a stand here, even though it's going to be unpopular. We socially conscious writers sometimes need to take a risk for our art.

I would like to say that any guy who thinks he can run ACROSS CANADA clearly has a screw loose. For one thing, the chafing! And the blisters! It just seems awful. I don't believe someone would choose to run that far. Still, every September, every kid in every school everywhere in Canada has to run something like a tenth of how far Terry Fox ran as a reminder that there's no such thing as dreaming too big.

Along with everyone else, I had to join in the Terry Fox Junior High Terry Fox Run last week. Of course, it was raining that day, but there wasn't any point in putting on a rain jacket. I was just going to be sweaty inside the jacket anyway. I envied the kids with notes excusing them from physical activity. It wasn't the first time that I wished I could be hit lightly by a car, just enough that my ankle fractured or something. Only the athletes like the run. The rest of us suffer through, except that group that seems to have some secret route where they get to sit under a tree for an hour and saunter in later.

The course was the same last year: a lap around the field, then into the community. What started off as a mass huddle turned into a long string that snaked through the streets of Calgary. *Four* different old ladies yelled at us in four different languages. I can only assume that they were not words of encouragement as we turned their perfectly manicured lawns into mudholes and trashed their flowers and hedges. It didn't take more than a few feet before my lungs started burning with every inhale and I wanted to spit every few paces. I don't know where all that saliva comes from, but it never goes away. By the time the school was in sight, we were drenched with sweat and rain and ready to be done. But NO! We had to go around the stupid field again. By the time I got inside, the hot chocolate that was being given away had run out, and it was time to get to the next class.

Do I feel better about myself for running the Terry Fox Junior High Terry Fox Run? No. Do I feel like I've done something for the community? Maybe I would have, but I only got donations from two people. So what do I know? I know that Terry Fox was one tough dude. One tough, maybe crazy dude.

Hi, Artie!

I'm not going to lie: I chuckled at some parts of your rendition of the Terry Fox Run. I didn't realize you felt so strongly about a national icon. I wanted something a little more positive about the experience, so I'm going to shorten your article and get Kennedy to write something to complement your piece. Two opposing viewpoints would be interesting to readers.

Mr. E

Dear Mr. Everett,

I think you misunderstood my piece. I'm not against Terry Fox or even what he stands for in Canada. I just think there are better ways to show our support for his goal than running around a field once a year. If you let me have my own column, I bet that would come through in a clearer way.

Yours truly,
Arthur Bean

▸▸   ▸▸   ▸▸

From: Kennedy Laurel (imsocutekl@hotmail.com)
To: Arthur Bean (arthuraaronbean@gmail.com)
Sent: October 7, 22:22

Hi Arthur!

How's it going? SO...I heard something VERY INTERESTING about you tonight! My mom invited Robbie and his dad and brother to come over for Thanksgiving dinner, and when we were talking before dinner, I realized that you and your dad were probably alone for Thanksgiving and I felt TERRIBLE! So I told Robbie and HE mentioned that I shouldn't worry about it because you and your dad were going to have curry buffet at YOUR GIRLFRIEND'S HOUSE!!!!!!!!
   You NEVER mentioned having a girlfriend! So you'd better tell me EVERYTHING! LOL! I want to hear all about her! I can't BELIEVE that you never mentioned her before! Robbie said that you hang out with her ALL THE TIME! EVERY day in class I ask you what's new and you NEVER ONCE even hinted that you had a girlfriend! You're so WEIRD LOL!! I can't wait to meet her!

Kennedy ☺

▶▶   ▶▶   ▶▶

October 7th

Dear RJ,

34

Kennedy knows about Anila, but I can't tell if she's mad or excited when she uses so many exclamation points.

Plus, it's even weirder because Thanksgiving dinner was so strange. For one thing, Anila's parents are really quiet. My dad and I got there, and he had brought a bottle of wine, so he gave it to Mr. Bhati, who was all confused. "Oh. We don't drink, but you're welcome to have a glass if you like," he said. Then my dad was all embarrassed and declined, but Mr. Bhati put the bottle in the middle of the table, like a constant reminder of my dad's mistake.

Anila looks exactly like her mom. They both have thin eyebrows that look like they've been painted on, and puffy cheeks and pointy chins. If I ever marry Anila, I'll know what she's going to look like when she's old. That's so weird I don't even want to think about it ever again.

The worst part of dinner was that the food was crazy spicy, and we couldn't leave right afterward. I barely ate anything except the bread, but my dad ate a bunch and complimented Mrs. Bhati with every bite. That was embarrassing enough, but then afterward, he kept having to go to the bathroom, and then he came back and tried to make jokes about us not being used to fancy Indian spices. I don't think he was trying to be racist, but I was so embarrassed I couldn't even look at him. Every time my dad got up, there was this horrible silence and Mr. Bhati was just staring at me, and Mrs. Bhati was searching for something to say to keep the conversation normal. We ended up talking about camp for a really long time, especially since Anila's parents are good friends with the owners.

Anila must want to break up with me by now. I guess I'll find out soon.

Yours truly,
Arthur Bean

▶▶   ▶▶   ▶▶

From: Kennedy Laurel (imsocutekl@hotmail.com)
To: Arthur Bean (arthuraaronbean@gmail.com)
Sent: October 8, 10:58

Hi Arthur!

How was dinner with your girlfriend??? My Thanksgiving was REALLY weird, because my brother and Robbie's brother got into some kind of stupid FEUD about a video game or something (you'd THINK that my brother would let it go because he's in college! He's SO immature!).

Do you wanna hang out? You can tell me ALL about your ROMANCE LOL!!! I'M DYING of suspense here LOL LOL!!! I'm SO bored and I'm stuck here with my brother, and he's totally hungover and is lying on the couch watching lame sports!

Kennedy ☺

From: Arthur Bean (arthuraaronbean@gmail.com)
To: Kennedy Laurel (imsocutekl@hotmail.com)
Sent: October 8, 11:13

Dear Kennedy,

I can't believe I never told you about Anila. I'm sure I did. Maybe you weren't listening, because I definitely would have talked about her, although I guess I don't see you one-on-one at school very often. She has a good singing voice. When she asked me if I wanted to be her boyfriend, I figured, why not? She's really into world music and documentaries, which is cool too.

As for this afternoon, I can't come, but I would love to! We are going to Nicole's house because she and her boyfriend invited us for dinner. Can we hang out another time?

Yours truly,
Arthur Bean

From: Kennedy Laurel (imsocutekl@hotmail.com)
To: Arthur Bean (arthuraaronbean@gmail.com)
Sent: October 8, 14:02

Hi Arthur!

Anila sounds cool! I can't wait to meet the girl who stole your heart LOL! Definitely we'll hang out soon! Plus, Robbie was talking about your movie at Thanksgiving and I TOTALLY think it sounds like it will be AWESOME! He said that it was like *Watchmen* meets *The Avengers* meets

Survivor meets *Zombie Apocalypse* meets *The Bachelor* LOL!!! Sounds INTENSE!! I learned SO MUCH about you! Robbie was telling me about how much trouble you guys got into at camp! It sounded HILARIOUS! I didn't know you were such a BADASS, Arthur! He told me about how you guys would sneak out at night and go light fires on the beach and go swimming and steal food from the mess hall and never get caught!

Kennedy ☺

⏩   ⏩   ⏩

> Hey, Robbie: I got an email from Kennedy saying you told her stuff about camp. What did you tell her? We made a deal never tell anyone.

> u mean the camera? of cours i didnt tell her. u r so para-noid.

> But what DID you tell her? Other than stuff about Anila.

> I TOLD HER NOTHING. CHILL. what r u worryed about? its gonna be fine. well use it and return it b4 anyone even notices.

▶▶   ▶▶   ▶▶

From: Arthur Bean (arthuraaronbean@gmail.com)
To: Anila Bhati (anila.i.bhati@gmail.com)
Sent: October 8, 16:58

Dear Anila,

How are you? I hope you're good. My dad is going to call your mom to thank her again for last night's dinner, so I thought I would let you know. I really liked all the food. Your mom is a good cook! Can you send me some of the recipes she made? I'm going to try them at home myself.
    Anyway, thanks for dinner.

Yours truly,
Arthur Bean

From: Anila Bhati (anila.i.bhati@gmail.com)
To: Arthur Bean (arthuraaronbean@gmail.com)
Sent: October 8, 19:30

Dear Arthur,

I'm so glad to hear from you! I was so worried that you would literally break up with me because my parents are so weird! I can't believe that my dad wouldn't say anything, and I told my mother to make sure that the food was not too spicy, and then I think she made it extra spicy just to spite me! It's adorable that you're lying about liking it though. You're so polite!

I'm supposed to start volunteering with this group that is trying to get shark fin soup banned from restaurants, and I think the orientation is this week. Plus, I'm going to see a play on Sunday during the day. So I don't know if I'll have time to see you, which is so very terrible! I wish we went to the same school. Then we could at least see each other.

Anyway, I'll call you tomorrow after school! Miss you!

Anila
XOXO

▶▶   ▶▶   ▶▶

Assignment: Using Symbolism

Many authors use symbolism to emphasize major themes or predominant emotions in their work. Symbols can take the form of an object, as we read in "The Painted Egg Cup"; weather, as we read in "Lightning Storms over Flin Flon"; or characters, as in "A Funeral for a Clown." Adding symbolism can enhance your story immensely. Practice adding symbolism to your work by writing about an event in your own life. Focus on an object or a type of weather to symbolize how you felt in the moment.

Due: October 12

From: Kennedy Laurel (imsocutekl@hotmail.com)
To: Arthur Bean (arthuraaronbean@gmail.com)
Sent: October 10, 10:03

Hi Arthur!!

We should TOTALLY hang out this weekend! Maybe your girlfriend can come too! I am DYING to meet her! I want to know what kind of girl wins the heart of the infamous Arthur Bean LOL!

Kennedy ☺

▶▶   ▶▶   ▶▶

Assignment: Using Symbolism

by Arthur Bean

At camp, I felt like I was carrying around a giant bar of really heavy soap. At first, I had the soap with me because I'd never been away from home before, and especially not for so long. I emailed my dad and my cousin Luke whenever I could, though the counselors limit it, so we can be "in the moment" when we're at camp. And when I heard back from them, it was like I used a little bit of the soap, and it got a little bit smaller. I had the soap with me all the time in our cabin too because I wasn't sure if Robbie was going to be nice to me, but then he was, so that used up a little bit of the soap too. Each time I did something new, the soap felt really heavy, but then when I was done, it felt a little smaller and lighter. It was heaviest before big things, like sneaking out at night to go swimming or getting up in front of a bunch of people to read a poem I wrote about my mom. Sometimes I didn't do things because the soap weighed me down, but the smaller it got, the easier it was to do new things.

I still have some of the soap, but it's small now.

Arthur,

I believe you are using soap as a symbol of your fear without saying as much. It's difficult to get to the bottom of your piece, as it feels quite opaque. You're on the right track, but next time, try setting up the symbolism in a more transparent manner and thinking carefully about what works well as a symbol. Could you have chosen something more fitting to your setting or your emotion?

Ms. Whitehead

Ms. Whitehead,

I think the bar of soap is very symbolic. After all,

weren't you the one telling us about some kind of Shakespeare scene about washing your hands?

Arthur Bean

▶▶   ▶▶   ▶▶

October 13th

Dear RJ,

RJ, I'm going to confess something, but you can't tell ANYONE!! OK...here goes. Robbie stole a video camera from arts camp. They had a whole room of equipment we got to use. We made the best movies with this one camera. It has to be worth at least $1,000. Once Robbie told me that, I was nervous even to hold it. But it was awesome that we got to actually use it. Then, on the last night of camp, I accidentally helped Robbie break into the equipment cabin to take it. We had snuck out, and he told me to keep a lookout for people. I thought he was just going to take a leak beside the building, but then he came out with the camera. He said we could return it next year, since no one is even at the camp the rest of the year except the owners. I told him not to do it, but he said I was being a baby.

RJ, I was an accidental accomplice! I never wanted to be a criminal. I did want to be cooler, and hanging out with Robbie makes me feel like I'm a cooler guy.

43

Plus, we had been doing all these dares at camp, so stealing the video camera was like one more dare. And Robbie doesn't want to keep it forever. It was just so that we could have a good camera for our movie. But we still have it, and I think we probably shouldn't have taken it, and now I don't know how we can get it back. I mean, it's big. It's got all kinds of cool lenses that we can attach, and it has a tripod and stuff. Robbie threw out most of his clothes just to get it in his bag!

Maybe Tomasz and Halina haven't noticed that it's gone, but I know where it is all the time. Every time I hear a siren on the street (which is a lot!), I think that the cops are coming to arrest me. And I didn't really do anything! I mean, Robbie is the one who stole the camera, technically. I'm just holding on to it for him. It just sits at the back of my closet right now, since Robbie can't have it at his house.

I'm innocent here! But I think sometimes the innocent feel guilty too. I just wish that we could get rid of it, but Robbie thinks we need it for our movie. If we don't have it, the whole thing will suck.

I had to tell someone! Sometimes I can't sleep from the knot in my stomach.

Yours truly,
Arthur Bean

▸▸   ▸▸   ▸▸

Robert and Arthur,

It has come to my attention that you gentlemen have been working on a video project that utilizes school property without any teacher supervision. From here on in, I will be a part of your production meetings. I will be available to help with anything you need, including script work, equipment needs, and ensuring that you have no challenges working within AV Club guidelines. We'll meet next week to begin crafting the film.

Mrs. Ireland

▶▶   ▶▶   ▶▶

AV CLUB GUIDELINES

1. Any student may join the AV Club.
2. All equipment must be reserved ahead of time and signed out upon use and signed in upon return.
3. Have fun!

▶▶   ▶▶   ▶▶

can u believe Ireland? shes gonna treat us like were kids

I know. I bet she won't even let us do the scene where the zombies all end up in the equipment shed and then get ripped apart by rabies-infected dogs.

Lame

Wait... Do you think she'll have to see the camera? It's got the arts camp sticker on the case! Maybe we should try and return it.

just leave the case at home. I doubt she has 2 b there 4 acctual filming. its fine!

▶▶   ▶▶   ▶▶

October 18th

Dear RJ,

I don't know if it's just me, but Kennedy seems to be around a lot more this year. She's different too. I mean, she's still Kennedy, but now she's like Kennedy Plus. I wish I could explain it better. It's awesome, but I don't know why she's different.

She even started passing me notes in French class. They don't say anything much, but she's a super-talented writer so they're hilarious. I hope that she can make our movie have some good one-liners. I'm really good at writing drama, and Robbie writes emotion and tension really well, so I think she'll be in charge of making it funny. Not funny all the time though, just at the right moments. It's really kind of cool. Last year I saw her talking to all her friends all the time, and now I'm the one she's talking to. I bet there are some guys out there who totally wish that they were me.

Yours truly,
Arthur Bean

▶▶   ▶▶   ▶▶

Hey, Artie!

The Drama Club is hosting a spooky haunted house this year as a fund-raiser for costumes. It's an evening event over the three days around Halloween, and Mr. Tan is really hoping to get lots of people to come and check it out. They've put a lot of planning into the different classrooms having different themes. Could you interview a few of the students involved in the haunted house and write a piece that helps

*them garner interest? That is, unless you're
too afraid...*

Mr. E

▸▸   ▸▸   ▸▸

From: Anila Bhati (anila.i.bhati@gmail.com)
To: Arthur Bean (arthuraaronbean@gmail.com)
Sent: October 19, 18:00

Dear Arthur,

I can't believe that I won't get to see you this weekend!
I miss you so much that my heart aches... I was telling
my mother, and she said that it's good to miss someone
and that it gives you the opportunity to appreciate them
more. Do you think so? I was even thinking that I would
quit the shark group so that I could hang out with you!
What do you think? I could finally get a chance to beat you
at Scrabble—make up for that time you won! (Don't mind
me... I have a competitive streak.) I also miss Pickles! I
want to snuggle your cat again. She's so cute!

Anyway, let me know. I can cancel the shark group
meeting on Saturday if you want to do something.

Love,
Anila
XOXO

From: Arthur Bean (arthuraaronbean@gmail.com)
To: Anila Bhati (anila.i.bhati@gmail.com)
Sent: October 19, 19:24

Dear Anila,

It would be nice to see you, but I don't want you to quit your shark group for me! I'm really busy, and I have to put aside some time to work on my novel, but maybe we can do something as well. If you do cancel your meeting, I'm sure we could find something fun to do. I like your idea of playing Scrabble. I do enjoy kicking your butt at board games. ☺

Just kidding, of course. Let me know what you want to do, and I can see if my dad will drive me wherever. Also, I don't know why you think Pickles is cute. I'm starting to think that she hates all guys. She's the opposite of a misogynist cat. A misterogynist?

Yours truly,
Arthur Bean

▶▶   ▶▶   ▶▶

my bro is haveing a party for halloween cuz my dad will be away. oct 27. u coming?

The party sounds awesome! Maybe I can ask my dad if I can sleep over.

sure. bring chips and coke tho.

I guess I should start planning my costume. Do you think people would get it if I went as Stephen King?

I could dress like a king with a crown and cape and stuff, and a name tag that says Hi, My Name Is Stephen.

No 1 will get that. its stupid

▶▶   ▶▶   ▶▶

ZOMBIE SCHOOL

by Arthur Bean and Robbie Zack

October 23 Production Meeting Notes

It's imperative to start by establishing the world of your movie. Where does it take place? When in time is it set? What has happened before the movie begins to get the plot moving? Write down your brainstorming ideas and identify your work by marking your initials beside your comments. —Mrs. Ireland

SETTING:
Zombie School ovioussly takes place in our school in northeast Calgary. —rz

Or in a school that is actually a cruise ship, which

would add to the tension, because no one could get off the boat. —AB

Its not going to be on a boat. —rz

It could be on a boat. —AB

If they were on a boat, then how would they get the horrible virrus that took over the world and turned adults into zombies? that has to hapen for the hole movie to make sense. —rz

Fine. No boat. But we need the school to look like it's been abandoned because all the teachers came down with the zombie plague—like a horror movie school, with lockers ripped apart, graffiti everywhere, and a teacher playing a zombie walks down the hall, eating part of a person. —AB

And the teachers could be hiding in a den in the basment of the school. —rz

Because there are vampires and werewolves on the second level! —AB

No —rz

You can't say no in a brainstorm. —AB

You can if its a stupid idea. —rz

You're going to be the first person eaten by a zombie on-screen. —AB

My caracter is going to be so powerfull that his karate chops sever heads with 1 blow. —rz

My character is going to have superhuman strength and be able to rip apart zombies with his pinky finger. —AB

My caracter is going to have the power to move things tellle-pathcally. But anyway, do you think Mr. Tan will be the head zombie? Hed be the best at it, being the drama teacher. —rz

I thought Ms. Whitehead should do it. It's important that there are women who have roles they can sink their teeth into. That's what Anila says. —AB

"Sink their teeth into"? Zombies? Vampires? Get it? —AB

lame —rz

I suggest that you both spend some time before our next meeting focusing on what is APPROPRIATE for a school-related film project. —Mrs. Ireland

▶▶   ▶▶   ▶▶

October 23rd

Dear RJ,

I think our movie is going to be epic! We've been

working really hard on it, and it sounds like it's going to be just like a Hollywood film. I even think that Robbie might have been right about the video camera. The ones in the AV Club are so old that this one is going to be way better! All we need is to get Mrs. Ireland on board. At our next meeting, we're going to tell her that she can't stifle our creative outlet, or else we'll start smoking. I bet she believes that.

Yours truly,
Arthur Bean

▸▸   ▸▸   ▸▸

October 21

Flying Spirits Arts Camp
Box 13, RR1
Canmore, AB

Dear Camper,

We are writing to you with some distressing news. We have recently completed our inventory, and it has come to our attention that one of the video cameras has gone missing from the camp's AV center.

As a premier arts camp, we pride ourselves on having quality equipment for our campers to use. As you know, one of the principles of the camp is honesty and integrity, in both creative work and moral character. We are devastated to think that one of our summer campers has broken this moral code and taken some of our shared equipment. Should this camera and its accompanying pieces not be found, we will be forced to raise campers' registration fees to cover the cost of this equipment.

We had hoped that the camera was merely misplaced, but we conducted a thorough search and nothing has turned up. As such, we are making a plea to all our summer campers: should you have any information about the missing equipment and its whereabouts, please let us know.

Sincerely,

Tomasz Zloty
Director, Flying Spirits Arts Camp

▶▶   ▶▶   ▶▶

Robbie, did you get that camp letter?

wat letter?

They know about the camera!

i never get any mail

This is NOT mail you want! Anila got a letter too. They're totally onto us. I had to play so dumb with Anila.

well u can be reelly dumb sometimes

▶▶   ▶▶   ▶▶

October 24th

Dear RJ,

We're so screwed. I got a letter in the mail from the camp about the missing video camera. They must know it was me and Robbie! They have to! Why else would they say that if I had any information I should come forward?

I bet they only sent it to the suspects. They sent one to my dad too, and he brought it up at dinner. I acted really shocked. I was going to act outraged that someone would do that, but I didn't want to overdo it (that's something we learned at arts camp—when you're acting, don't be too over the top). He didn't say much more, so I think he believed me. (Another reason to thank arts camp, and another reason that I don't want to get caught.)

This is why I don't break rules, RJ. I ALWAYS get caught. People who always break the rules know how to do it.

I can't handle it.

Yours truly,
Arthur Bean

▶▶   ▶▶   ▶▶

My dad said I can sleep over on Saturday. I didn't tell him it's a party though. Also, can I maybe invite Anila for the evening? I think I should, because she is my girlfriend.

I also think I will go as Leonardo da Vinci. I'll wear paint on my clothes and a bandage over my ear!

u come up with the dummest costumes. wear my old batman costume. bring anila if u want. and dont forget the chips.

▸▸   ▸▸   ▸▸

October 26th

Dear RJ,

I'm going to my first actual party tomorrow night. Anila is coming with me too. It'll be our first outing as a couple. I don't know what to do at a party. For one thing, Robbie's brother doesn't even seem to like me, so I don't know what his friends are going to be like. Robbie said that Caleb invited half his grade to the party. I can't imagine how they're going to fit that many people into their apartment. I wonder if there's going to be a beer keg. I don't know how people even get beer kegs, but parties on TV always have beer kegs. Especially teenagers. They ALWAYS have kegs.

Anyway, I'm kind of nervous, RJ. I don't like big crowds and I hate being hot. They don't even have a balcony to use to cool off. I also don't want Anila and Kennedy to meet. Sometimes Anila can be really weird. When she gets nervous, her voice changes. She sounds almost Australian when that happens. I don't even know why I invited her. I wanted her to come, but as soon as I invited her, I started thinking about how she and Robbie were always arguing at camp and how I'll have to introduce her to everyone and probably talk to her all night because she won't know anyone else. I think that I might hate going to parties.

Yours truly,
Arthur Bean

▶▶   ▶▶   ▶▶

I'm so excited for the party tonight, Arthur. I can't wait until you see my costume! XOXO

What time does it start? We should probably get there early.

> You're right. We'll pick you up at 6. That way we can help Robbie and Caleb decorate and set up.

> My first party! I'm so glad you'll be there by my side. I'm already a little nervous... XOXO

> PLEASE don't be nervous!

▸▸   ▸▸   ▸▸

From: Kennedy Laurel (imsocutekl@hotmail.com)
To: Arthur Bean (arthuraaronbean@gmail.com)
Sent: October 28, 2:13

Hi Arthur!

Can you BELIEVE that party?!?! Robbie was SO out of line!! I can't BELIEVE he said those things about MY brother!! You NEVER talk about someone's FAMILY like that! What a total jerk!! I'm never speaking to him AGAIN! And he's one to talk! Caleb is the STUPIDEST, LAMEST person around! That was seriously the worst party EVER!

ANYWAY, enough about the terrible party! It was nice to FINALLY meet your girlfriend LOL! She seems really REALLY REALLY nice! And her costume was...ummm... detailed LOL! She talks A LOT. I think she talked to

EVERYONE there (but I guess that wouldn't be hard when there's only 6 people LOL!). ANYWAY, seeing you with your girlfriend made me kind of sad, because I miss having a boyfriend! Too bad you're taken ☹ LOL! I guess I'll just make do having you be my friend! OK, I'm getting sleeeeepy. Bedtime! See you on Monday!

Kennedy

▶▶   ▶▶   ▶▶

From: Anila Bhati (anila.i.bhati@gmail.com)
To: Arthur Bean (arthuraaronbean@gmail.com)
Sent: October 28, 7:20

Dear Arthur,

Thank you so much for the invitation to Robbie's party. You looked really cute as Batman. I hope my Frida Kahlo costume wasn't too over the top. I can't believe no one knew who I was! It's too bad that more people didn't show up. Robbie's brother looked so disappointed, didn't he?

One thing though. I didn't think that you were still friends with Kennedy. Don't get me wrong. She seemed quite nice, but she was all over you, hugging you and giggling at everything you said. Even when she and Robbie got into that terrible argument about their brothers, she was touching your arm as though you were on her side. I was watching and you never told her to stop or anything. I didn't want to seem like I was jealous or anything, but it seemed quite strange. She knows that you're my boyfriend, right? She barely talked to me. She seemed to talk only to you. I thought parties were for meeting new people and learning from them. Anyway, I guess if she's a friend of yours, that's OK, but can you make sure she knows that you have a girlfriend and that girlfriend is me?

I probably sound mad. I'm not mad at you (how could I be?) but I thought about it a lot last night, and I felt you should know how I felt.

XOXO
Anila

▶▶   ▶▶   ▶▶

October 28th

Dear RJ,

Well, the party was an epic fail. Robbie's brother had invited a whole bunch of people, but barely anyone came. There wasn't a keg either. And the people who came were super bored. There were two girls other than Kennedy and Catie and Anila, and they spent the whole time on their phones and then they left really early. Also, there wasn't any food except the chips I brought, and Robbie said that his brother was going to order pizza, but then no one had any money, so we didn't get anything.

Then there was this huge fight between Kennedy and Robbie. Kennedy made a comment to Catie about Caleb having no friends and throwing a lame party, but Robbie overheard her and freaked out. He started saying all this mean stuff about her brother, and she got super upset and left. It was the strangest thing. I've heard both of them say rude stuff about their own brothers, but then they were super defensive about their families. I don't understand it.

I also spent the whole night wishing I hadn't invited Anila. She was talking to everyone about "being green" and no one seemed to care. It was kind of embarrassing, but I couldn't tell her not to do that. She was even trying to tell Caleb about composting or something. Then today Anila's mad at me for hugging Kennedy. But I had nothing to do with that. Kennedy has never hugged me, and then last night, she hugged me when I got to Robbie's, and again later when I got her a glass of water, and then AGAIN when she left (although I think that one was more to annoy Robbie than anything else).

I don't get girls. And I was right. Parties are definitely not my thing.

Yours truly,
Arthur Bean

▶▶   ▶▶   ▶▶

Haunted Hoopla at Scary School

by Arthur Bean

Do evil clowns, chain saws, or vampires set your teeth on edge? What about all of them together? Then you'd best stay away from Terry Fox Junior High around Halloween, because the school is about to get spooky!

As a fund-raiser, the Drama Club will be taking over part of the ground floor of the school to create one of the biggest haunted houses in the city. For three nights, the school will transform into a ghostly lair, with each room along the drama hallway boasting its own scary theme. I spoke to Mr. Tan and some of the Drama Club kids to get a sneak peek into what kinds of horrors their house will hold, but most of them were tight-lipped. "It will be epic," one kid promised me. He and his friend laughed (rather maniacally). "There will be a lot of blood and gore. Buckets of blood. And gore," said one girl.

Mr. Tan just smiled at this reporter and said that people would have to come to find out but that the house was not for the faint of heart or small children. Afterward, I did some investigative journalism to get you, my fair readers, the full story. Based on what I could find hiding in various classroom storage rooms, as well as props hidden in the theater dressing rooms, I believe that haunted house goers will probably find scarily themed rooms like:

Chemistry gone wrong! A mad scientist leads you through his lab, showing you his crazy...textbook collection.

Some sort of crazy man-beast named Mop Man and his sidekick, Dustpan Dave, hiding out in the janitor's closet after escaping the freak show at the circus.

Math.

This reporter is scared already. The haunted house runs from October 30 until November 1 and costs $5 per person, or $4 with a food bank donation.

Come…if you dare…

Great work, Artie! I'm not sure how much of this you've imagined, but I think you've done a good job of creating interest. Make sure you fact-check your stories; we don't want to lead our readers on. You never know when someone may have an intense Mop Man phobia!

Cheers!
Mr. E

▶▶   ▶▶   ▶▶

From: Anila Bhati (anila.i.bhati@gmail.com)
To: Arthur Bean (arthuraaronbean@gmail.com)
Sent: October 29, 16:17

Dear Arthur,

Are you avoiding me? I haven't heard from you in a few days, and I'm worried about you! I hope you didn't think I was mad at you! I had a lovely time at Robbie's house, and I promise I'm not one of those jealous girls who doesn't allow her boyfriend to have friends who are girls. I'm not like that. I guess I was just surprised that you are friends with a girl like Kennedy. She's so different from us.

Anyway, I really want to talk to you! I miss you so much, and it's been AGONY thinking that you were mad at me for my email. I didn't mean to make you mad! I'm so sorry!

XOXO
Anila

From: Arthur Bean (arthuraaronbean@gmail.com)
To: Anila Bhati (anila.i.bhati@gmail.com)
Sent: October 29, 18:08

Dear Anila,

I'm not mad at you! You shouldn't think that. I've just been busy with my movie and school. I meant to write you back on Sunday when I got your email.

Kennedy is just like that. She's nice but we're just friends. I'm just sorry you didn't get a chance to talk to her, because of that fight and all. She reads a lot too, like you!

Yours truly,
Arthur Bean

▶▶　▶▶　▶▶

October 29th

Dear RJ,

So it seems the ignoring thing that Luke suggested works! At first I just pretended like I never got Anila's email, so then she wrote again and was sorry for getting mad. I didn't think that would work at all, but it did! Does this work for everything? My mom always said that you should face a problem head-on, but I think she might have been wrong. It's a great trick! I'll never get in trouble again! I'm going to take Anila to the haunted house on Halloween to make sure everything's OK. Plus, it's in the dark, so nobody will even recognize us!

Yours truly,
Arthur Bean

NOVEMBER

November 3rd

Dear RJ,

I hung out with Anila today. She was really quiet. I was going to ask her what she was thinking about, but she does that to me all the time, even in the middle of movies, and I hate it. I don't know what to answer. I feel like she wants me to say that I'm thinking about her, but most of the time I'm not. I'm thinking about almost everything other than her.

Sometimes I am thinking about her, but then I think about whether she would have gotten along with my mom. I don't know if she would have. My mom got annoyed when she overheard people in the grocery store talking loudly about their opinions of stuff. She wasn't very quiet herself, so then she would turn to me and say things like, "I'm not sure that the middle of the store is the BEST place to share your old-fashioned opinions on union dues" (or whatever they were talking about). Sometimes she would get called out on it, and then she would pretend like she wasn't talking about that person. It was really embarrassing.

Anila talks loudly about her opinions. Sometimes it's like I can even hear my mom sighing and huffing in the kitchen, even though I know she's not there. It's funny how she was so loud herself, but then other loud people annoyed her so much. I miss her, RJ. She would have a good title for our movie. She was good at making up titles for things.

Yours truly,
Arthur Bean

▶▶   ▶▶   ▶▶

ZOMBIE SCHOOL

by Arthur Bean and Robbie Zack

November 6 Production Meeting Notes

I'd like to see a recap of what you decide as a team during these production meetings, as well as any notes that you feel are important to remember in future meetings. Note any questions and requests in your production meeting notes, and I will respond accordingly. I expect that the AV Club meetings will be productive and respectful and that material will remain appropriate at all times. —Mrs. Ireland

MEETING RECAP:
We definitely need access to the school roof to do the alien parts of the movie. Hopefully we can rent

a crane to get a good shot of a spaceship. We know you probably don't have the budget for it, but if you do, that's number one. We also need access to the basement for the scenes when we discover the secret lair of the zombies. We probably need access to the whole school because we could put the camera in a corner so it looks like a security camera shot of us discovering the zombies. Which means that we also need a green filter so we can make it look like security camera footage.

TO REMEMBER:
I want there to be a scene where Ms. Whitehead is watching the news in a mall electronics store and there are zombie outbreaks in New York and Chicago and Dubai. All around her are dead bodies. She is laughing. Mr. Lee comes up behind her. Now he is also a zombie, and he holds her hand. They kiss, and then they start chewing on each other's faces. It'll be super gross. —AB

i think we should keep the romantic senes between reel peopl, cuz 2 teachers are never gonna kiss, even to be famous. —rz

I think they would to be famous. Everyone wants to be famous. —AB

not for eating faces. —rz

I still think we should log it as an upcoming scene in the movie. —AB i guess it could come after the alien sene. maybe mr lee gets sucked into the spaceship as its happenning, and his eyeball could be stuk between Ms. W's teeth as it pulls away. —rz

Gentlemen, there will be no filming on the roof or in the basement. It's not written currently in the AV Club guidelines, but it is a strict rule governing the club. And a crane is most certainly too pricey for the club budget. Finally, a romantic interlude between "teacher zombies" will not occur. —Mrs. Ireland

▶▶   ▶▶   ▶▶

AV CLUB GUIDELINES—Amended

1. Any student may join the AV Club.
2. All equipment must be reserved ahead of time and signed out upon use and signed in upon return.

3. Have fun!
4. Filming must take place in sanctioned school areas. There is no filming in areas restricted to students, such as the basement, the roof, and the staff room.

▶▶   ▶▶   ▶▶

Assignment: The Gratitude Project

This year, our school is participating in a citywide initiative called the Gratitude Project. It is a yearlong program designed to help us all recognize the contributions we make to other people's lives, and to thank those who have helped us. We'll be doing short projects during the year to contribute to this project, culminating in a public art display in the downtown library!

Our class will be starting the Gratitude Project with letters to veterans for Remembrance Day. Please write a thank-you letter to a veteran. You may wish to focus on a freedom in your life that you are particularly thankful for, which may come in the form of an event, a person, or even an object that has changed your life.

Due: November 13

▶▶   ▶▶   ▶▶

November 9th

Dear RJ,

I just had the best night! Kennedy and I had a history project to do, so she asked if I wanted to do it together! Then she came over! Instead of working, we just ordered pizza and found old monster movies to watch online. It was super fun. And there was this one time when Kennedy said that she was getting scared, and she hid her face in my sweater. She was laughing the whole time, so I just put my arms around her and I said, "I'll save you from the monster, my darling!" and we cracked up. She was practically cuddling with me. I doubt she noticed, but I noticed. I didn't want to move in case she moved away.

It was a whole different feeling than when I'm with Anila. Anila sits really close and kind of pushes herself into my side, but it's really comfortable. It's like how I used to sit close to Mom—like I know she's there and I expect her to be close by. Anila used to sit like that at campfire too, and that was good because it was cold out.

But enough about Anila. Tonight was all about Kennedy sitting close to me. It feels so different. I'm so aware of her. Even when she isn't in sight in a room, I know exactly where she is. It's like my Spidey sense is tuned to her frequency. If I were a super-hero and she were a super villain, I would totally be able to find her and defeat her in battle. She would never be able to hide from me.

Yours truly,
Arthur Bean

▶▶　　▶▶　　▶▶

> I was thinking we could hitchhike to camp and pretend to be lost in the woods and then while we're there, we could put the camera back. Maybe we could go next weekend?

> R U CRAZY?!?! were u listening at all to the storeys at camp? hitchhikers GET KILLED ALL THE TIME.

> No. The hitchhiker WAS the killer. And we won't kill anyone. We'll just return the camera.

> how about u just leave it in ur closet? its fine. they cant see ur stuff u kno. we r not getting killed over this thing!

▶▶　　▶▶　　▶▶

From: Anila Bhati (anila.i.bhati@gmail.com)
To: Arthur Bean (arthuraaronbean@gmail.com)
Sent: November 11, 16:09

Arthur, remember when you told me that you were "very busy this weekend" and "couldn't hang out"? And then when I talked to you just this morning, you said that you were "studying all day for a test"? Don't you find that very, very strange, since I saw you today at the mall with Kennedy...

I know you said that you guys are just friends, but decent guys don't ditch their girlfriends for their "just friends." I don't know what you were doing at the mall, but it sure didn't look like studying. It looked like you were sitting in the food court laughing and eating fries with Kennedy and a bunch of girls who look like Kennedy. Care to explain?

Anila

From: Anila Bhati (anila.i.bhati@gmail.com)
To: Arthur Bean (arthuraaronbean@gmail.com)
Sent: November 11, 22:12

Dear Arthur,

Avoiding your phone doesn't make things go away, you know. I've been so upset all day, and all I want to do is talk to you, and you won't answer your phone!

Anila

From: Arthur Bean (arthuraaronbean@gmail.com)
To: Anila Bhati (anila.i.bhati@gmail.com)
Sent: November 11, 22:20

Dear Anila,

I wasn't trying to avoid you. I promise! I'll explain:

I was at the mall today, but I was there with Nicole because she wanted a second opinion on what she should get Dan for his birthday. I was home alone, because my dad had a yoga thing. He called it a sound meditation. Does that mean there is sound or there isn't sound? I have no idea, but either way, it sounded a bit weird, so I didn't ask any more questions. Anyway, he was at yoga all day, and I WAS studying, but then Nicole came to my apartment and said that we should go to the mall. I saw Kennedy and her friends when Nicole was in the bathroom, and they called me over to sit with them while I waited. I was only there for a little bit. Then I left with Nicole and went back home.

I promise that I didn't ditch you! Well, maybe I did, but not on purpose, and not to go to the mall.

I have to go to bed now, but I'll call you tomorrow. Don't be mad anymore. ☺

Yours truly,
Arthur Bean

From: Anila Bhati (anila.i.bhati@gmail.com)
To: Arthur Bean (arthuraaronbean@gmail.com)
Sent: November 11, 22:38

Dear Arthur,

Thanks for writing back. I guess I shouldn't jump to conclusions, but at the same time, it sure seemed weird! I feel so foolish, being upset before knowing the full story. I'm not mad anymore. ☺ I do wish you had told me that you were going out with Nicole though. I just like to know where you are and what you're doing. I miss you when you're not around!

Love,
Anila

▸▸   ▸▸   ▸▸

Assignment: Dear Veteran

by Arthur Bean

Dear Veteran,

Happy Remembrance Day! I hope you're having a great day and that it is sunny outside. I mostly hope it's sunny outside for you since I've seen how they make you march down the street and stand at attention for a really long time, even though you are really old. It must be terrible to have to do that when it's raining, especially after you've been through a war. You probably feel like you shouldn't have to do anything you don't want to do after that. I think that's how I would feel.

Quick question for you: Did you find it really hard to be at war and still have a girlfriend? Did you have any girl problems when you were away? Did your wife or girlfriend want to know where you were all the time? How did you handle that? I bet you had to keep a lot of secrets too, so that you could win the war. That must have been hard on you. But you had to do it, right? For your friends and family to be safe.

Anyway, I wanted to thank you for fighting in the war for me. I mean, I know you weren't actually fighting for *me personally*, but I got a lot out of it. For one thing, my mom told me once that chocolate bars were invented for the war. So I'm pretty thankful that you wanted chocolate bars badly enough to invent them. Those are pretty awesome. And I think that duct tape was invented for you too, which is helpful, because my dad is terrible at fixing things, but duct tape is really good at fixing things. We've had one leg of our couch duct taped on for almost a whole year, and it still is standing. But I do mean it when I say thanks!

Yours truly,
Arthur Bean

Arthur,

Your letter could use some revising to make it more relevant and heartfelt—I'm not sure about your purpose here. I recognize that your sense of humor can be quirky, but it's important to recognize when humor is appropriate. Also, remember that not all veterans are senior citizens; soldiers who fought in recent military conflicts like Afghanistan are also veterans.

Ms. Whitehead

▶▶   ▶▶   ▶▶

From: Kennedy Laurel (imsocutekl@hotmail.com)
To: Arthur Bean (arthuraaronbean@gmail.com)
Sent: November 14, 7:32

Hi Arthur!

I just woke up, but I had the STRANGEST dream that I had to tell you about LOL! I dreamed that we were DATING LOL! It was so weird though, because my dream had parts of your movie in it too, so we were kind of in the movie, but we were kind of not in the movie, but we were also kind of making the movie! It's so hard to explain! Dreams, right? LOL! Anyway, we were running away from these zombies but there was a movie camera there, and when the director (who was Ms. Whitehead in my dream) yelled, "Cut!" we stopped running but we were STILL holding hands! And it was super exciting, but all I could think was, "I'm sure that Arthur has a girlfriend," and then just as I was about to ask you, I woke up! Isn't that CRAZY?! What do you think it means?

Kennedy ☺

From: Arthur Bean (arthuraaronbean@gmail.com)
To: Kennedy Laurel (imsocutekl@hotmail.com)
Sent: November 14, 8:03

Dear Kennedy,

I think it means you want a part in the movie. ☺ I guess that's why I'm so tired today. I was running through your head all night.

Yours truly,
Arthur Bean

From: Kennedy Laurel (imsocutekl@hotmail.com)
To: Arthur Bean (arthuraaronbean@gmail.com)
Sent: November 14, 8:06

LOL! LOL!! OMG Arthur! That is HILARIOUS!!! I'm laughing so hard right now! It's going to be an AWESOME day! Every time I get mad about something, I'm going to think about this and laugh! LOL!
   You are AWESOME!

Kennedy ☺

▸▸   ▸▸   ▸▸

Hi, Arthur! My school has a dance next Friday and I can bring a guest! Will you join me? XOXO Anila

Of course, it's my boyfriend duty! Do I have to dress up? I don't have anything except the suit I wore to my mom's funeral. But I'd rather not wear that.

No dress code! Just come looking handsome, as always! XOXO

I'm so pleased that you can come! I can't wait for you to meet my friends! This is going to be an amazing night! XOXO

▸▸   ▸▸   ▸▸

November 18th

Dear RJ,

Robbie told me today that his mom is trying to get full custody of him and his brother, which is weird because I didn't even think his parents were totally divorced yet. Robbie's super worried, but I don't think there's any way a parent can move her kids to another country. That's never going to happen. Although I guess things would be different if she knew about the camera. Now no one can know. Ever. I hope it's worth it. This movie is going to have to be amazing.

Yours truly,
Arthur Bean

▸▸   ▸▸   ▸▸

ZOMBIE SCHOOL

by Arthur Bean and Robbie Zack

November 20 Production Meeting Notes

CHARACTERS:
A good film is carried by strong and complex characters. Focus on your cast of characters this week, and provide a recap of what you decide.
—Mrs. Ireland

CAST RECAP:
We definitely are going to have a cast of teacher zombies. Then there's going to be a Good Guy Army called the GGA. There will be me and Robbie and then two love interests, and one guy who betrays us to the bad guys, but then he gets killed by zombies. There will be more people in the army too, but they don't have speaking roles.

There will also be a group of humans who are working against the GGA because they are stupid and they believe that zombies just need to be loved to turn back into real people. They are called Zombies Are People, but they call themselves ZAP.

Then we need a bunch of extras to play bodies and extra zombies and maybe werewolves if we decide to put them in. Then there might be some aliens who get in the way too, but they won't be real people. We're going to CGI them into the movie afterward.

We've decided that we don't need to hold auditions, because we don't want to have everyone in the school show up and then have to sit through bad auditions. So instead we'll just ask people to be in our movie who we think will do a good job.

TO REMEMBER:
My caracter will be awesome at karate and have a machine gun that blows people apart at the seems. —rz

My character will be named Zipcode, and he's the leader of the GGA. —AB

I think my caracter will be the leader cuz I have a louder voice than you. —rz

OK, your character can be the leader at first, but then when the traitor to the GGA leads the GGA into the mall at night as a trap, your character will almost die and maybe get a leg or arm ripped off and then my character will take over as leader. —AB

And then my arm gets replaced with a bionic arm that has a built-in gun and all kinds of other usefull stuf. —rz

81

There is no need to add more violence to your film; excessive violence is unnecessary. You should also be fully aware by now of the school's strict policy against guns, real or imagined, in work produced at Terry Fox Junior High. —Mrs. Ireland

▸▸   ▸▸   ▸▸

AV CLUB GUIDELINES—Amended #2

1. Any student may join the AV Club.
2. All equipment must be reserved ahead of time and signed out upon use and signed in upon return.
3. Have fun!
4. Filming must take place in sanctioned school areas. There is no filming in areas restricted to students, such as the basement, the roof, and the staff room.
5. There will be no guns in the film, and other weaponry will be kept to a bare minimum.

▸▸   ▸▸   ▸▸

i ran into kennedy and her stupid bro at the mall today. i thot he was gone for school. that family sux. Hes such a turd.

Well, maybe he's not the greatest person, but Kennedy is pretty nice. I don't know why you're mad at her. It's not her fault who her brother is.

shes the 1 who called my bro a looser 1st. bad jeans run in the family. wanna come over? i got a new game.

Yeah. I'll be there in 30. And it's genes. Jeans are pants.

keep that up and ur JEANS will make a great wedgie...

▶▶   ▶▶   ▶▶

Assignment: Creating an Effective Setting

Having a strong feeling of place helps to ground stories for the reader. Knowing more about the setting can bring your reader into the world you are creating. The short story we studied, "A Girl's Guide to Prairie Winters," is an excellent example of using place to engage readers. Write a short paragraph about a room in a house using adjectives, details, and descriptive language. What can we learn about the inhabitants of the space from the decor?

Due: November 26

▶▶   ▶▶   ▶▶

November 23rd

Dear RJ,

HUGE NEWS, RJ. HUGE! I can't believe what has happened to me!

After school, Catie came up to me and handed me this note from Kennedy. And the note was all about how she's been too shy to tell me but that she likes me and she thinks it's not just as a friend. She knows that I have a girlfriend and that I love Anila, but she just thought I should know that she thinks of me as more than a friend. Then she said that she doesn't want me to break up with my girlfriend for her because she would be upset to know that she was the reason I broke up with Anila, so I should just stay with Anila and never mind anything that the note said.

What???

Now I have to go to the dance tonight with Anila! How am I supposed to do that?!?

Yours truly,
Arthur Bean

▶▶   ▶▶   ▶▶

November 24th

Dear RJ,

I went to the dance with Anila yesterday. I tried not to think about Kennedy the whole time, and so I focused really hard on Anila and being nice to her friends.

On the way to the school, her dad asked me, "What's new?" and the only thing I could think of was Kennedy, so I tried to talk about school stuff, but then every second sentence seemed to start with "Kennedy and I" and I could tell that Anila was getting upset about it. So then I stopped talking, and just let Anila talk about the Environment Club and their next big outing.

I met her friends. (I think they're hippies. They wore really long clothes that didn't really fit, and two of them had dreadlocks!) She didn't have as many friends as I thought she did. I thought she was really popular, like Kennedy, but she's not. Her school is way different than mine too. It still looks like a school, but she calls all her teachers by their first names. Anila seemed so excited to introduce me to people, so I met all her teachers and they said stuff like, "It's nice to finally meet the famous Arthur. I've heard a lot about you." I guess she talks about me a lot. I don't think I've ever talked about Anila at school. We danced, even though I'm a pretty terrible dancer, but no one made fun of me. That was kind of cool, since barely anyone dances the fast songs at my school; they're all just waiting for the slow songs. Even the teachers were dancing, and they were allowed to bring their husbands and wives, and some of them did.

Now it's the weekend, and all I can think of is Kennedy again. Maybe I'll call and ask Luke what to do. He always has the best advice.

Yours truly,
Arthur Bean

▶▶ ▶▶ ▶▶

Hi, Arthur, best boyfriend ever! I just woke up! All that dancing last night must have tired me out. I had such a wonderful time! All my friends said that you're awesome, which I knew already...

Having you at my school yesterday was one of the nicest things ever. I wish so much that I could see you every day. Don't you wish that too?

I'm already counting the days until I see you again. I miss you, Arthur Bean! XOXO

Yeah, last night was fun. Your school is so different than mine! Have a good weekend!

▶▶   ▶▶   ▶▶

From: Kennedy Laurel (imsocutekl@hotmail.com)
To: Arthur Bean (arthuraaronbean@gmail.com)
Sent: November 25, 19:41

Arthur!

Why haven't you responded to my note! I thought you would AT LEAST call me this weekend or something, and you didn't say ANYTHING!! Maybe I don't mean anything to you, even as a FRIEND!!!

Kennedy ☹

From: Arthur Bean (arthuraaronbean@gmail.com)
To: Kennedy Laurel (imsocutekl@hotmail.com)
Sent: November 25, 20:38

Dear Kennedy,

Of course you mean a lot to me! It's just that your note said that I didn't have to respond, so I didn't. Are you really upset? I'm sorry. I was at a dance with Anila this weekend, and I spent a lot of time talking to my cousin Luke, which my dad said was expensive because it was long distance, so I wasn't allowed to call anyone else.

Yours truly,
Arthur Bean

From: Kennedy Laurel (imsocutekl@hotmail.com)
To: Arthur Bean (arthuraaronbean@gmail.com)
Sent: November 25, 20:59

Hi Arthur!

I just think we should talk about this! I know I can't really ask you to do that because I'm NOT your girlfriend, but I can't HANDLE having this drama between us!!! I HATE knowing that you hung out with Anila this weekend! It makes me so sad!!

Kennedy ☹

From: Arthur Bean (arthuraaronbean@gmail.com)
To: Kennedy Laurel (imsocutekl@hotmail.com)
Sent: November 25, 21:29

Dear Kennedy,

I don't want any drama between us either! I'll talk whenever you want to, and I promise I won't mention Anila. This is between you and me, right? No one else. Don't be sad. ☹

Yours truly,
Arthur Bean

▸▸   ▸▸   ▸▸

Assignment: Effective Setting:
The Lloyds' Bathroom

by Arthur Bean

Lloyd Lloyd spent a lot of time in the bathroom, more than the average human, which meant that he liked to have things to look at while he was there.

It was a pretty average bathroom, as far as bathrooms go. There were two sinks side by side, both white. The counters on either side of the sinks showed whose sink it was. The right one was filthy, covered in tiny moustache and nose hairs from Lloyd's shaving, along with dried splotches of toothpaste around the sink, the counter, and the mirror in front of it. The second sink was pristine, since Lloyd's wife, Betsy, only cleaned up her side. Her counter space was covered with tiny bottles of lotions and makeup, mostly filched from hotels. The towels were mint green, matching the mint-green paint. It was very minty in there and reminded Lloyd to brush his teeth. The mint green was only broken up by the number of framed pictures on the walls. There was the poster of kittens their daughter gave them as a Christmas present when she was ten, found on sale at Walmart. There was his college degree, which merited a place here because he felt that his education was being thrown down the toilet. An engineering degree, and all he did was work at the bank as a teller. Then his wife's decorative plates were there, and a watercolor of some castle, and a black-and-white photograph of trees. Lloyd liked looking at the trees the best, so he put that one right in front of the toilet, along with a framed page out of a Where's Waldo? book to give him something to do.

Lloyd finished up and flushed the toilet. He ran his hands under the water, more to avoid his wife nagging him about washing his hands than to actually wash them. He turned and wiped his hands on the mint-green towels. The towel rack was unreasonably far away from the bathtub, according to Lloyd, although he now had to look at the hole in the drywall from when he had tried to move the rack closer and failed. He would have to try again in the spring.

He opened the door and yelled, "Bets! You need to tone down on the chipotles next time you make chili!"

The End

Arthur,

I was worried about where you were going to take this piece, but you've done a nice job describing the Lloyds through your description of the bathroom. It's a little crude, but I appreciate that you mostly stayed away from the obvious jokes and focused on the assignment.

Ms. Whitehead

▶▶   ▶▶   ▶▶

> i thot of a great name 4 my caracter. BLAZER.

> Like a jacket?

> no morron. Like Lazer and Blade put 2together.

> Oh, I get it. Cool!

▶▶ ▶▶ ▶▶

November 27th

Dear RJ,

I think Kennedy might be avoiding me. I told her we could talk, but every time I see her at school and try and bring it up, she says that she can't talk to me about it and runs away. I thought about asking Catie what's going on, but I don't know if she'll tell me the truth anyway. I don't know what I should do. Luke said that I should take Kennedy out on a date and see what happens. He said that if I go out with Anila and Kennedy back-to-back, it'll be clear what I should do, because I can compare them easier. He's a smart guy!

Yours truly,
Arthur Bean

▶▶   ▶▶   ▶▶

From: Arthur Bean (arthuraaronbean@gmail.com)
To: Kennedy Laurel (imsocutekl@hotmail.com)
Sent: November 27, 21:06

Dear Kennedy,

What are you doing on Sunday? Maybe you would like to go to Heritage Park and see the Christmas town.
    I have two free passes that I cut out of the newspaper.

Yours truly,
Arthur Bean

From: Kennedy Laurel (imsocutekl@hotmail.com)
To: Arthur Bean (arthuraaronbean@gmail.com)
Sent: November 27, 21:49

Hi Arthur!

I would LOVE to go to Heritage Park!! It's one of my favorite places to go!
    How did you know?! You must know me so well LOL!!

Kennedy ☺

From: Arthur Bean (arthuraaronbean@gmail.com)
To: Kennedy Laurel (imsocutekl@hotmail.com)

Sent: November 27, 22:00

Dear Kennedy,

That's great!
    Can your dad drive us there? My dad can pick us up.

Yours truly,
Arthur Bean

▶▶   ▶▶   ▶▶

Robert and Arthur,

Please welcome Von Ipo to the AV Club!
He's expressed an interest in working on
your zombie project, and I think he will be
a great addition to your creative team. He
comes with extensive experience in making
short home movies, and he tells me that he
is well versed in editing software and film
design. He'll be joining our AV Club meetings
beginning next week.

Mrs. Ireland

▶▶   ▶▶   ▶▶

From: Von Ipo (thenexteastwood@hotmail.com)
To: Arthur Bean (arthuraaronbean@gmail.com)
Sent: November 28, 18:43

Hey, Artie!

So stoked to be in the movie. Can't wait to work with you guys—been writing movies and stuff since I was basically born. Anyway, just thought I would tell you how happy I am to do this. If you need suggestions of what movies to watch that I think would work well for what you are trying to do, let me know. I mean, I've probably seen a movie directed by every single director ever, so I'm good at giving suggestions.

I also have some suggestions for my character—was thinking it would be best if my character has a dark past. Like maybe my dad was a zombie hunter but was killed by zombies when I was a kid. Or my twin sister was turned into a zombie and I feel guilty cuz I led her into the zombie lair. I also think that my character should be the lead in the military. I'm in army cadets and have been since I was old enough to be in it, so I'm basically a soldier. I would be able to do my own stunts too, because I'm really fit and flexible and can basically jump over anything from standing up.

Von

▸▸   ▸▸   ▸▸

I just got the most annoying email from Von. Can we cut him from the movie before I actually turn him into a zombie?

give him a chance. he was in Romeo & Juliet with me last year. he's pretty funny.

plus he probly knos how to use our camera better than us.

I doubt it. I don't think we should even show him that camera. He'd probably rat us out.

Besides, he probably already has the best camera ever made ever. EVER.

well if he does we wont need the other 1.

I was being sarcastic.

ur so funny I forgot to laff.

▶▶　　▶▶　　▶▶

From: Von Ipo (thenexteastwood@hotmail.com)
To: Arthur Bean (arthuraaronbean@gmail.com)
Sent: November 29, 8:04

Hi, Artie!

I've got more ideas for you! Every great movie needs to have a romance going on, and I think that my character probably grew up next door to one of the girls. Then we lost touch, but we see each other and fall in love again. Then her character dies at the end. That's what every good action movie has. I've basically seen them all, so I know how to write good dialogue and great plot twists.

Von

▶▶　　▶▶　　▶▶

Hi, Arthur! I was thinking that we should go to Heritage Park on Saturday. They have a wonderful Christmas display in the old town. It's quite magical, if you've never been! XOXO

I also have a coupon for two free passes. That leaves us more money for hot chocolate and treats… XOXO Anila

Sounds good. Can your parents drive us?

▶▶   ▶▶   ▶▶

November 30th

Dear RJ,

I did what Luke suggested and I'm going out with Anila on Saturday and with Kennedy on Sunday. We're even doing the same thing both days, so I'll really know what I should do after I've done the identical activity! And it's not really a date with Kennedy. After all, I'm going with Anila first, so that definitely counts for something! And there's no way that I will run into Anila there on Sunday (who would go twice in one weekend?), so she won't know that I'm out with Kennedy. I don't want her to worry or get jealous or mad. It's not like I've done anything. Kennedy and I are just going to hang out and talk.

Yours truly,
Arthur Bean

DECEMBER

December 2nd

Dear RJ,

What a weekend! I went out with Anila yesterday to Heritage Park, and I had the chance to find all the best spots so that when I went with Kennedy today, I could show her the cool stuff. Kennedy was so impressed that I knew Heritage Park so well! Plus, I bought tickets for the hayride for me and Anila, and then we didn't have time to go on it, so I got to use those with Kennedy and I'm sure she thought I was such a good date for having bought the tickets ahead of time. Little did she know!

But that's not what was great, RJ. The great part was that I got to kiss Kennedy!!!

When we first got there, I didn't know if I should bring up the fact that she told me she liked me, or if she would do it, and I think she didn't know what to do either. So we were walking through all the old houses and stores, and looking at the Christmas stuff, not really saying anything. It was getting weird, so I started telling her facts about Heritage

Park and all the old houses and stuff, but she interrupted me and said that she was getting cold. So I asked her if she wanted hot chocolate, but she said that I needed to keep her warm. So I asked her how, and she hugged me, and then we stopped walking (because it's really hard to hug someone and keep walking). Then Kennedy pulled away a little bit and she said, "Are you going to kiss me?" and I didn't know what to say, so I said, "I don't know. I have a girlfriend." So then Kennedy said, "I know, but it's so romantic here."

And it was AWESOME. It was so romantic, and everything was perfect, and I forgot about Anila totally, and we kissed and then we held hands (well, mittens) and we walked through the park and took the hayride along the reservoir and got hot chocolate, and we were one of those couples that people smile at when they see them because we were so in love. I wanted to kiss her again, but I didn't get a chance to because my dad was already waiting for us when we left the park.

I don't know what I'm going to do about Anila now, but today I'm not going to worry about anything, because I KISSED KENNEDY!!!

Yours truly,
Arthur Bean

▶▶   ▶▶   ▶▶

December 2nd, well actually December 3rd

Dear RJ,

I can't sleep, for two reasons. One is that I feel kind of terrible for kissing Kennedy when I'm dating Anila. Good guys don't do that, and I hate feeling guilty. The second reason is that I keep thinking about Kennedy and how I might get to kiss her again. I don't know what I'll do if she's all over me at school tomorrow!

I think I should probably keep my weekend free in case Kennedy wants to hang out again though. Or maybe I should make her jealous and tell her I'm busy. I don't know which would be better.

I can't tell Robbie. He'll be so mad if he hears that Kennedy is in love with me. Things have gotten so weird between him and Kennedy since their fight. It gets worse every day, so I know he's going to think that I'm on the enemy's side. I've been trying not to get into whatever they're fighting about though, because I guess he's my best friend now. That's a weird thing to say, especially since I worry that he might beat me up at any time. Well, not beat me up, but he could definitely stop being my friend and go back to making fun of me. Especially with all that stuff with his mom. I looked it up to see how long custody cases last, and all the stuff I found said that it could be months or even years long. It was all people writing in the States though, so maybe it's faster in Canada. It must suck to not know what your parents are doing. One thing I know for sure, my parents would have never gotten divorced or separated or whatever. They were way too geeky for that.

Yours truly,
Arthur Bean

▶▶   ▶▶   ▶▶

Hey, Artie,

We're focusing on the winter break in the next issue, and I'm hoping that our keen reporters (like you!) have ideas for what students could do during the holidays. If you have an idea for an article highlighting something in the city that might be interesting to other kids, let me know!

Mr. E

▶▶   ▶▶   ▶▶

ZOMBIE SCHOOL

by Arthur Bean and Robbie Zack and Von Ipo

December 4 Production Meeting Notes

Focus on creating one central conflict for your movie. What is *the* driving force behind the story? Remember to include everyone's opinions as well as a list of things to remember for the next meeting. —Mrs. Ireland

MEETING RECAP:
Obviously, the central conflict is the one where the GGA has to take down the teacher zombie army while simultaneously fighting ZAP, and possibly werewolves and, if we can figure it out, aliens. Meanwhile, there will be some infighting in the GGA because there's a member of the GGA who no one wants to be there, but he just invites himself into the gang and they don't know how to get rid of him. Also, one of the GGA gets kidnapped by ZAP and gives away classified information after getting tortured, so the GGA end up in a standoff with ZAP and one of the soldiers dies. There's also a mole working inside the GGA, but he betrays them once and then he dies in a zombie fight. Then there's a scene when he's a zombie, and the GGA has to kill him, but they don't really want to because he was one of them even though he betrayed them in the end.

TO REMEMBER:
We should make ZAP a group of vampires! —VI

That's the lamest idea I've heard in a long time. This is a serious movie. Vampires have no place in serious movies. —AB arties rite. its not a romance. —rz

We can't just add in every mythical creature ever imagined. What's next? Centaurs? Hippogriffs? —AB

u should talk. u want aliens in EVERYTHING. —rz

I bet I could get my dad to rent a crane for us. He's really good friends with the guy who built the whole university. —VI

Note the amended AV Club guidelines in regard to crane rentals. —Mrs. Ireland

▶▶   ▶▶   ▶▶

AV CLUB GUIDELINES—Amended #3

1. Any student may join the AV Club.
2. All equipment must be reserved ahead of time and signed out upon use and signed in upon return.
3. Have fun!
4. Filming must take place in sanctioned school areas. There is no filming in areas restricted to students, such as the basement, the roof, and the staff room.
5. There will be no guns in the film, and other weaponry will be kept to a bare minimum.
6. All equipment must be provided by

the students or the drama department. Any additional equipment must
be requisitioned through the AV Club
administrators.

▶▶   ▶▶   ▶▶

From: Von Ipo (thenexteastwood@hotmail.com)
To: Arthur Bean (arthuraaronbean@gmail.com)
Sent: December 4, 17:04

Hi, Artie!

Great meeting today! Can't wait to start filming, right?
Totally happy to help film scenes that I'm not in too. I
really understand the complexities of filming something.
I'm basically an amateur expert.

I've done editing too. My brothers and I have made
probably more than 100 movies that we sent in to
America's Funniest Home Videos. Totally almost won
once too. They called us and told us that our home video
was the funniest movie they had seen in over ten years,
but that we couldn't win because we weren't over twenty-
one. But they basically told us that we would have won like
ten times because our stuff was so funny.

Can also help you with special effects. I've been playing
around in my spare time with computer animations, and
basically I can pretty much make anything happen. So
when you need to make the school explode and stuff, I
can do it for you, no problem!

Let me know. Happy to hang out and show you a few cool things on my computer if you want to learn how the pros use the camera. It might make the movie look less amateur.

Von

▶▶   ▶▶   ▶▶

From: Arthur Bean (arthuraaronbean@gmail.com)
To: Kennedy Laurel (imsocutekl@hotmail.com)
Sent: December 6, 16:20

Dear Kennedy,

I'm writing about Heritage Park for the newspaper article this week, since we had such an amazing time! I bet people don't know that you can get two hot chocolates for the price of one if you order a large and two cups! And they probably don't know that you can squeeze two people into the one front seat of the hayride beside the driver if you sit really close together. Do you want to write it together? We could make it really cute.

Yours truly,
Arthur Bean

From: Kennedy Laurel (imsocutekl@hotmail.com)
To: Arthur Bean (arthuraaronbean@gmail.com)
Sent: December 6, 23:41

Dear Arthur,

I've been thinking about you a lot and I wanted to tell you something!

First, I had a GREAT time with you at Heritage Park last weekend! But I know you have a girlfriend and I don't want to break you guys up! I think that I shouldn't have kissed you! I thought that maybe I should, but I feel TERRIBLE about it now! I know I should talk to you in person, but it's so hard! I like you A LOT, but let's just be friends, OK?!

Kennedy ☺

▶▶   ▶▶   ▶▶

From: Anila Bhati (anila.i.bhati@gmail.com)
To: Arthur Bean (arthuraaronbean@gmail.com)
Sent: December 7, 18:09

Hi, Arthur!

I would love to see you tomorrow or Sunday. I really miss you, and Heritage Park was just so lovely last weekend. It made me wish dearly that I could see you all the time. Don't you wish that too? If only we went to the same school… Maybe I'll switch at winter break so that we can see each other every day. Wouldn't that be so wonderful? Then I could be in your movie too! I probably don't live in the right school district though. Oh, how these imaginary borders keep us apart!

XOXO
Love,
Anila

From: Arthur Bean (arthuraaronbean@gmail.com)
To: Anila Bhati (anila.i.bhati@gmail.com)
Sent: December 7, 18:30

Dear Anila,

I think you would hate my school. The teachers use so much paper and I bet that half of them don't recycle.
　　But that's too bad. It would be fun to have you in the movie.
　　I don't think that I can hang out this weekend. I've got loads of homework, plus I promised Robbie that I would work on the movie. We've got a lot to do if we want to start filming in the new year!
　　I miss you though. I'll call you tomorrow!

Yours truly,
Arthur Bean

From: Arthur Bean (arthuraaronbean@gmail.com)
To: Kennedy Laurel (imsocutekl@hotmail.com)

Sent: December 7, 19:21

Dear Kennedy,

I totally understand what you mean. It's really hard to be together, and I know that I'm really busy. But don't worry. I'll always make time for you! That's really nice that you don't want me to break up with Anila. I know that would mean a lot to her.

I would love to hang out with you this weekend if you're free. (I'm supposed to see Anila on Saturday. She's very in love with me.)

Oh yeah, and did you talk to Robbie? He was talking about you the other day and I think he's really sorry about the whole fight thing. Maybe you guys can be friends again, especially if we're going to be hanging out more!

Yours very truly,
Arthur Bean

From: Kennedy Laurel (imsocutekl@hotmail.com)
To: Arthur Bean (arthuraaronbean@gmail.com)
Sent: December 7, 21:08

Hi Arthur!

You should DEFINITELY keep your plans with your girlfriend this weekend! I don't want to get in the way of TRUE LOVE!! I hope you get that we shouldn't have kissed! It was not right at all!

Also, I REALLY am not talking to Robbie! He was SO

MEAN to me! Catie said that he's been a jerk to lots of people.

What's his DEAL?!?

Kennedy ☺

From: Arthur Bean (arthuraaronbean@gmail.com)
To: Kennedy Laurel (imsocutekl@hotmail.com)
Sent: December 7, 21:14

Dear Kennedy,

I'm sorry! I shouldn't have brought it up. I just want you guys to be friends again. Did you know that his parents are actually getting divorced soon? Before they were just separated, but now it's all being finalized. That's got to be really hard on him! Plus, his mom is being really weird, and his brother is being a jerk. I know he wants to apologize, but you know Robbie.

And trust me, I know we're only friends. I just hope that we can be best friends!

Yours truly,
Arthur Bean

From: Arthur Bean (arthuraaronbean@gmail.com)
To: Anila Bhati (anila.i.bhati@gmail.com)
Sent: December 7, 23:06

Dear Anila,

It turns out that I am free this weekend. Do you want to do something still?

Yours truly,
Arthur Bean

▶▶　　▶▶　　▶▶

> my mom is maybe moveing back to canada. she says my dad is 2 rapped up in work 2 b a good father.

> and wed probly have to eat real food again. i think her bf broke up w/her. probly cuz shes bossy.

> Maybe your parents will get back together after all! It happens in the movies.

> i hope not! at least it means I only have 1 more xmas in north carolina

▶▶　　▶▶　　▶▶

From: Kennedy Laurel (imsocutekl@hotmail.com)
To: Arthur Bean (arthuraaronbean@gmail.com)
Sent: December 13, 18:20

Hi Arthur!

You'll never BELIEVE what happened to me! I got detention LOL! I guess that will teach me to ask Fiona for a pencil DURING a pop quiz LOL! LOL!! It wasn't so bad though! Von was there too for being late for school three days in a row! He had to promise to buy an alarm clock LOL!! He's so cute and so tiny! He reminds me of a Pomeranian puppy LOL!!! And he talks so much LOL! Did you know that he's visited like thirty countries ALREADY?!?! ANYWAY, Catie just ditched me, so do you want to go to a movie tomorrow?!?

Kennedy ☺

From: Arthur Bean (arthuraaronbean@gmail.com)
To: Kennedy Laurel (imsocutekl@hotmail.com)
Sent: December 13, 18:28

Dear Kennedy,

I can't believe you would get in trouble. You're way too cute for that! But I can believe that Von was there. That guy can be so annoying. I bet he annoys teachers so much that he barely gets detention because they don't even want to see him anymore!

I'm absolutely up for a movie tomorrow night. Your pick!

Yours truly,
Arthur Bean

▸▸   ▸▸   ▸▸

From: Anila Bhati (anila.i.bhati@gmail.com)
To: Arthur Bean (arthuraaronbean@gmail.com)
Sent: December 14, 14:02

Hi, Arthur!

Are you going to wish me a happy birthday? I can't believe
you haven't said anything. I assume it's because you have
a surprise planned for tonight! (I can smell a surprise a
mile away. Ask my parents! I always know!)
    See you tonight!

XOXO
Love,
Anila

From: Arthur Bean (arthuraaronbean@gmail.com)
To: Anila Bhati (anila.i.bhati@gmail.com)
Sent: December 14, 15:23

Dear Anila,

Shoot! You figured me out! I asked a bunch of people to

go to the movies with us tonight! A lot of people couldn't make it though, and some other people bailed at the last minute because of the snow. But Kennedy can come, and she's so excited to see you again, and Robbie really wanted to come but his mom is in town.

Anyway, we're going to come over and get you at 6 tonight.

Better get ready!

Yours truly,
Arthur Bean

▶▶   ▶▶   ▶▶

December 14th

Dear RJ,

WORST EVENING EVER!

Apparently I forgot about Anila's birthday and I'd already told Kennedy I'd go to the movies. So then I had to go with both of them to the same movie. I kind of wanted to try that thing that you see in movies where you pretend like you're only there with one person, and then keep making excuses to get popcorn or go to the bathroom and stuff, and then go sit with the other person, but I'm pretty sure that would never work.

Instead, I pretended like it was Anila's birthday party. But I didn't want Kennedy to know that I had forgotten, so I just never said anything about it. Kennedy looked so shocked when my dad picked her up and Anila was already in the backseat. Anila seemed mad that no one else came with us, and Kennedy didn't talk to Anila either. Then the movie was sold out, and we had to sit around for an hour waiting for another movie to start.

I didn't know what to say to anyone. I was worried that they would figure out what was going on, and once, when Kennedy went to the bathroom, Anila turned to me and said, "I can't believe how self-centered she can be. She hasn't even wished me a happy birthday!" Then I had to agree, because AS IF I was going to tell her that Kennedy actually invited me to go on a date and she didn't even know that it was Anila's birthday! I don't even know what the movie was about I was so nervous the whole time! I'm just glad it's over!

Yours truly,
Arthur Bean

▶▶   ▶▶   ▶▶

From: Arthur Bean (arthuraaronbean@gmail.com)
To: Anila Bhati (anila.i.bhati@gmail.com)
Sent: December 15, 14:09

Dear Anila,

That was kind of a terrible birthday! Sorry about that. I

didn't know Kennedy was going to be so weird. I'll make it up to you. I'm also sorry that I forgot your present at home. I'll bring it to you next weekend. I hope that the rest of your birthday weekend goes better!

Yours truly,
Arthur Bean

▶▶　　▶▶　　▶▶

From: Arthur Bean (arthuraaronbean@gmail.com)
To: Kennedy Laurel (imsocutekl@hotmail.com)
Sent: December 16, 11:42

Dear Kennedy,

How's your weekend? How was your volleyball tournament? Did you guys win? I'm sure you did!

I wanted to say that I'm sorry about Friday night. Things got a little weird, but I didn't think you would mind so much. I mean, Anila is my girlfriend right now, so I kind of had to bring her along. I'm sorry about that though. I was really looking forward to hanging out with just you. I'll make it up to you! I'm going to get you the best Christmas present EVER!

Yours truly,
Arthur Bean

From: Anila Bhati (anila.i.bhati@gmail.com)
To: Arthur Bean (arthuraaronbean@gmail.com)
Sent: December 16, 21:06

Dear Arthur,

Thanks for apologizing. It was weird and awkward, wasn't it? The rest of my birthday weekend wasn't much better either. We had dinner at home and a birthday cake from Dairy Queen (although I do love ice cream cake!).

Anyway, I'm calling this birthday a fail. But that's OK. I should have many more…

I hope your weekend was productive. I spent quite a bit of time researching things, and I found us something really fun to do. It's called the Clean Water campaign. They clean the rivers and lakes and get the garbage out of the water. It's not until the spring, but then we can go together! What a crazy date, right?!? We would be garbage pickers together. The idea makes me laugh. I can already hear the funny things you would say about the different stuff we found.

I can't wait to see you this weekend!

XOXO
Love,
Anila

▶▶   ▶▶   ▶▶

ZOMBIE SCHOOL

by Arthur Bean and Robbie Zack and Von Ipo

December 18 Production Meeting Notes

After Christmas, we'll bring all the elements of your film together with the intention to film after spring break. Use this time effectively to flag any other ideas you would like noted before the task of scriptwriting begins.—Mrs. Ireland

I worked on a bunch of cool scenes for Tuff Arnold (my character) and added them to the production notes!—VI

Great. I'm sure they will add a whole level of excitement to the script and make the movie, like, the best thing EVER because you're so amazing at writing.—AB

we still havent really added the wearwolves. we should do that if were going to.—rz

VON'S SCENES:
There's a big zombie fight scene in the school cafeteria. Basically everyone is dead and the only living good guys are huddling in the corner, about to be eaten by zombies. Tuff Arnold (me) has been attacked by a zombie, and I'm bleeding and stuff. But I get up and I drop-kick the zombie's head off. The other zombies stop and look at me, and I say, "Get in line!" and I spin kick the zombies around me.

I turn to the good guys who were about to get eaten and say, "So...who wants to buy me lunch? I forgot my wallet...in that zombie's BRAIN!"

Then Tuff Arnold (me) is in the thick of the zombie war that has broken out in the school gym. It looks like the zombies are going to win, and then I have a brilliant plan. "Get out of the gym! I've got a plan!" I say to Mackenzie, who is in love with me. "No, Tuff! You can't do this! Don't do this! Think about us, Tuff!!!!" She is sobbing and grabbing on to my arm. Meanwhile, I'm killing zombies with the other hand. "I have to do this, baby. But remember that I loved you," I say.

I wait until all the zombies are in the gym and they are closing in on me. Then I reveal my secret weapon and yell "YOLO!!!!" and press the self-destruct button. The entire school blows up. The camera goes to Mackenzie, who is blown into the air by the force of the explosion but lands softly in a pile of hay. "He did it," she whispers. Then she smiles through her tears. "He really did it." The camera pulls back over the city, and the sun comes out (because it was raining before).

Credits roll.

▶▶   ▶▶   ▶▶

December 18th

Dear RJ,

I don't know what to do about Kennedy vs. Anila. Anila's so nice, and I like talking to her. And she likes me a lot. I don't want to hurt her by breaking up. I wish my mom were here. She would know what I should do about it. I've been trying to think of what she would say, but I don't even know anymore. It's like I don't really even remember what advice she used to give me. But here's the thing, RJ. I can't really be with Kennedy anyway, at least not until she and Robbie are friends again, so I need them to get over this stupid fight and make up, so that I can go out with Kennedy.

I'm caught in the middle, but if they were talking to each other, then Kennedy could work on the movie with us, and then I could tell her about the borrowed camera hiding in my closet. Instead, Robbie is totally rude to her whenever they are close to each other, and Kennedy and Catie say rude things back. It's mostly Catie who starts it, but Kennedy says stuff too. I've asked Luke what to do, but he has no idea either. I guess I have all of Christmas break to think of ways to get them talking.

Yours truly,
Arthur Bean

▸▸   ▸▸   ▸▸

Christmas Happenings: Hayrides, Hot Chocolate, and Heritage Park

by Arthur Bean

Looking for ways to make your holidays extra special for your sweetheart this year?

There are plenty of options around Calgary! The holidays are not just about the mall and great deals, but also about spending time with the people you love.

This reporter headed out to get the dirt on Heritage Park's Christmas event, but what did I find? A snowy wonderland that even the hardest hearts can't mock. There are wagon rides, crafts, fancy gingerbread houses to admire, carolers, and a general sense of merriment around the old historical village. Not to mention that the hot chocolate was really tasty, although a little expensive for this reporter, who thought it should be free.

Go soon though, since this is the last weekend it's open.

To make it an even cheaper day out, look for 2-for-1 coupons in the newspaper or online (not this newspaper, a *real* newspaper).

Hey, Artie!

This is great! I'm so pleased that you enjoyed your day there, and you've done a nice job summarizing what readers can expect if they go. A perfect addition to our last edition before the break (although we are a real newspaper; don't sell us short!).

Have a great break, unless of course, you're Santa Claustrophobic!

Cheers!
Mr. E

▶▶   ▶▶   ▶▶

From: Von Ipo (thenexteastwood@hotmail.com)
To: Arthur Bean (arthuraaronbean@gmail.com)
Sent: December 19, 16:52

Hey, Artie!

I've got even more scenes now! Those other ones took me basically 5 minutes to write. I can ask the teachers to be part of the movie too. They would make good werewolves. It would be amazing, and I'm really great at making people look like animals. I used to be in a theater group when I was a kid, and I basically did all the makeup for everyone, so I'm really good at making people look like animals. But if you want them to be in it, I'm basically the favorite student in the whole school, so I'm sure that if I ask them to be in the movie, they'll all do it.

Want to meet over the break? Can bring my laptop and show you that software!

Von

▶▶   ▶▶   ▶▶

From: Anila Bhati (anila.i.bhati@gmail.com)
To: Arthur Bean (arthuraaronbean@gmail.com)
Sent: December 20, 9:02

Dear Arthur,

It was so fun last night to hang out with you! I really loved the documentary. Did you? At least, the parts you saw? You were so cute when you fell asleep! I've never seen you fall asleep in a movie before; you must have been so tired.

Anyway, thanks again for the bubble bath. I love the smell of grapefruit. You didn't have to get me anything for Christmas, but it's nice that you did. I wish I could see you over the break, but we're going cross-country skiing. We're not leaving until Christmas Eve though, so maybe we can hang out before then!!

XOXO and love always,
Anila

▸▸   ▸▸   ▸▸

From: Kennedy Laurel (imsocutekl@hotmail.com)
To: Arthur Bean (arthuraaronbean@gmail.com)
Sent: December 22, 10:03

Hi Arthur!

I just wanted to say have a GREAT Christmas! We're leaving for Whistler today, which should be awesome, but I hope you have fun too! I know that Christmas can be super rough without your mom, so I wanted to tell you that I'll be thinking about you while I'm on the slopes!

Kennedy ☺

From: Arthur Bean (arthuraaronbean@gmail.com)
To: Kennedy Laurel (imsocutekl@hotmail.com)
Sent: December 22, 14:25

Dear Kennedy,

Thanks so much! That really means a lot to me. I think this Christmas will be better, knowing that you'll be thinking of me from so far away! I'll definitely be thinking of you too!

Yours truly,
Arthur Bean

▶▶   ▶▶   ▶▶

off to north carolina, its gonna SUCK. dont rite 2 much of the movie w/out me.

I may get so bored I write the whole thing. Don't kill your brother. I hear they have the death penalty down there.

no garantees.

I'm going to try and get the camera back to camp over Christmas, and then say that it was a Christmas miracle. Just letting you know.

haha. how r u gonna get there?
hitch a ride with santa???

Whatever. Have no fun in the USA!

no prob.

▶▶   ▶▶   ▶▶

December 22nd

Dear RJ,

Christmas is going to suck. I wish that Robbie and
Kennedy were here. And while I'm at it, I wish for
a million dollars. If I had a million dollars, Dad
and I could just go away to Whistler or Hawaii or
something, like everyone else does. I wish he would
think about me for once. If Dad could stop his stupid
fight with Auntie Deborah, we could go to Edmonton;
then at least I could hang out with Luke. And I wish
that I could put the camera back at the camp, since
I'm wishing for unreasonable things anyway.

Yours truly,
Arthur Bean

▶▶   ▶▶   ▶▶

From: Anila Bhati (anila.i.bhati@gmail.com)
To: Arthur Bean (arthuraaronbean@gmail.com)
Sent: December 23, 19:19

Dear Arthur,

I was so happy to see you today! We ate all the cookies you brought over, and they were delicious. Did you make them? My sister ate so many that I had to hide the last few from her so that I could savor them.

I also forgot to give you your present…

OK. I'm lying. I don't have your Christmas present yet. I've been looking everywhere. I wanted to get you something really perfect. You mean so much to me. I thought about writing you a poem or a story, but I write things down and then I think it sounds so silly or juvenile. I don't know how to write poems the way that you do. You're so creative and amazing, Arthur, and I feel bad that I didn't get you anything for Christmas! I'm so sorry for being the lamest girlfriend in the world.

Love always,
Anila

From: Arthur Bean (arthuraaronbean@gmail.com)
To: Anila Bhati (anila.i.bhati@gmail.com)
Sent: December 23, 20:21

Dear Anila,

I'm glad you liked the cookies. I made them with Nicole and her boyfriend. Dan's a chef at some fancy restaurant, so he did most of the baking. Nicole and I just ate the batter.

I don't need any presents from you just because of one stupid day in the year. I don't even like Christmas! Your email was so nice. It was all the present I need.

Have a great trip to Banff. I'll see you when you get back.

Yours truly,
Arthur Bean

PS: Your poems are awesome. They don't suck at all.

▶▶   ▶▶   ▶▶

From: Von Ipo (thenexteastwood@hotmail.com)
To: Arthur Bean (arthuraaronbean@gmail.com)
Sent: December 25, 10:41

Hi, Artie!

Merry Christmas, buddy! How's your break going? I've basically been playing hockey every day, especially since we have a huge tournament between Christmas and New Year's. Not that I need to practice, but it's good for the team if everyone is there, especially since I am basically the captain. If you're bored over the break, you should totally come and watch us play. It's basically the same as the NHL, but we're obviously a lot shorter. ☺

Anyway, I know Robbie is away, but I thought you and I could hang out and write more of the movie. You could come over here. My mom can make us lunch and we can write and then play video games.

Anyway, let me know. I've got some really good ideas about what should happen next in our movie!

Von

▶▶   ▶▶   ▶▶

December 25th

Dear RJ,

I was right. I hate Christmas. It started with Pickles throwing up all over the kitchen, and then I had to clean it up. She must have tried to eat the tree or something. Then we opened presents and Dad tried to be excited, but it was so fake. He gave me a Nintendo GameCube, but I hate video games. They're boring. I only play them with Robbie because he doesn't like to do anything else most of the time. But when I opened my present, I got really mad and then I yelled at Dad about how this Christmas sucked and that we should have gone to Edmonton because at least my family was there. Then I said that I thought Mom was the best parent, and then he started crying and apologizing. I felt so awful right away, but I was still really mad, and then I got mad that he was apologizing about it, but by then I felt mostly angry with myself for making him feel bad on Christmas. But I didn't know how to apologize,

RJ. So I only kind of said sorry. We basically avoided each other all day, but I did hear him on the phone with Auntie Deborah, and it sounded like they were apologizing, so maybe I'll get to see Luke soon.

I know that Dad is trying really hard to be like Mom, but he's not doing a very good job. I kind of wish he would stop and just be Dad again.

Yours truly,
Arthur Bean

▶▶   ▶▶   ▶▶

From: Von Ipo (thenexteastwood@hotmail.com)
To: Arthur Bean (arthuraaronbean@gmail.com)
Sent: December 28, 12:40

Hey, Artie!

Did you want to come over? Got some awesome stuff for Christmas. I basically got all the new video games that were the top-rated games this year. Some of them aren't even out yet in North America, I think. They're really cool, but some of them are way better with more than one player.

Von

▶▶   ▶▶   ▶▶

December 28th

Dear RJ,

This has to be the longest Christmas break of all time. I've read so many books, and I've even been looking at things we can put into the movie.

I think Robbie will like some of my new ideas. I really hope so. This film is my opportunity to show-case my skills as a screenwriter. It's important to be able to write across genres.

I'm glad Robbie will be home soon. Von keeps emailing me, and I don't want to hang out with him, so I've been trying the whole "ignore him and he'll go away" thing, but it's not working.

I actually sometimes feel bad about ignoring him, but, RJ, he drives me crazy, so I think it's for the best. Plus, I don't want to see all his top-end equipment. It just reminds me that I have top-end equipment too, but it's not actually *mine*.

Yours truly,
Arthur Bean

▸▸   ▸▸   ▸▸

> We're home, Arthur! I missed you so much! How was your Christmas? XOXO

Welcome back! Christmas was pretty boring. How was Banff?

It was all right. There wasn't a lot of snow for skiing, and my sister was super moody. But other than that, it was lovely. Except for the missing you part, of course!

I can't wait to see you! Are you still coming for New Year's Eve? My parents are having all my cousins over (and there are a lot of them!).

My mom is already cooking for a midnight feast!

I'll be there. My dad said he could drop me off at 6 and pick me up at 12:30. Does that work?

I'm so pleased that you're coming to meet my whole family. They hear about you all the time! I'm sure they will love you as much as I do. XOXO

▶▶   ▶▶   ▶▶

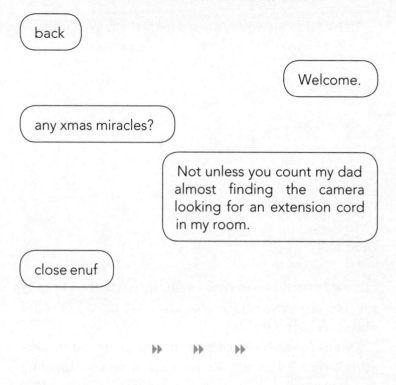

back

Welcome.

any xmas miracles?

Not unless you count my dad almost finding the camera looking for an extension cord in my room.

close enuf

▶▶   ▶▶   ▶▶

From: Kennedy Laurel (imsocutekl@hotmail.com)
To: Arthur Bean (arthuraaronbean@gmail.com)
Sent: December 31, 9:14

Hi Arthur!

How was your Christmas?? Mine was AMAZING!!! We skied SO much and I read some awesome books! Remind me to tell you about them! The hotel we were at was so nice too! There was a hot tub LOL! Anyway, what SUCKS is that my dad got a call and we had to come home for him to go to work today!

NOW I don't have ANY plans for NYE! ☹ Wanna come over and hang out??

Kennedy ☺

▸▸   ▸▸   ▸▸

December 31st

Dear RJ,

I know I should go to Anila's family party, but I really want to see Kennedy. Maybe she's changed her mind about us going out.

I want to see both of them, but Anila would under-stand, right? I mean, Kennedy has no one to hang out with tonight. And she asked me to come. She didn't even think that she would be in town, and New Year's sucks if you have to hang out by yourself. Anila has her whole family there. She probably won't even notice if I don't go. Man, RJ, it's times like these that I wish I had an identical twin...

Yours truly,
Arthur Bean

▸▸   ▸▸   ▸▸

Hi, Anila. I'm really really sorry, but I don't think I can come tonight. I'll make it up to you later though!

WHAT?!? Is everything OK? What happened?

Everything is fine, but it's kind of hard to explain.

Can your dad not drive you? because we can come pick you up and drive you home. I really want you to come tonight! It's going to be awful if you're not here!

It's not that. A friend got back into town earlier than she was supposed to and she's really upset about it and I need to hang out with her so that she feels better.

Are you hanging out with Kennedy?!?!

Just as FRIENDS! She's really upset!

You are seriously going to not come to your girlfriend's party because Kennedy is sad that her vacation is over?? I can't believe you.

Arthur, you suck! You really do. I'm so angry right now and I'm really sad…

I also don't really want to see you ever again. Actually, I don't think I ever want to even talk to you again. You are cruel, Arthur Bean.

No! It's not like that. I thought you would understand. You said yourself that New Year's Eve is a dumb holiday!

I mean, if you're that upset about it, I can come over to your house if you want. ☺

Don't bother. We're soooo done, Arthur. Go and hang out with Kennedy forever if you want!

▸▸   ▸▸   ▸▸

From: Arthur Bean (arthuraaronbean@gmail.com)
To: Kennedy Laurel (imsocutekl@hotmail.com)
Sent: December 31, 17:07

Dear Kennedy,

I can definitely come over tonight. I had other plans, but I canceled them. We'll have such a good time. I just have to tell my dad to drop me at your house instead. I can bring a bag of chips. I'll be there around 6:30, is that OK?

Yours truly,
Arthur Bean

From: Kennedy Laurel (imsocutekl@hotmail.com)
To: Arthur Bean (arthuraaronbean@gmail.com)
Sent: December 31, 17:17

YAY!!!! I'm SO glad that you're coming over!!! 6:30 sounds perfect!! My mom said that we can order pizza if you haven't eaten dinner yet LOL! Do you think you guys can pick up Catie and Jill on your way?!

Kennedy ☺

JANUARY

January 1st

Dear RJ,

This year is already weird, and it's only the first day. I went to Kennedy's house for New Year's last night, but she only talked to Jill and Catie the whole night and I ended up sitting on the couch watching TV with her older brother and little sister. She didn't even kiss me at midnight. I really thought she would! We were watching the ball drop and doing the countdown and everything, and when midnight hit, I turned to Kennedy, ready to give her the best kiss of her life, but she just hugged me fast and turned away.

Anyway, the whole thing was super lame, but I'm still pretty glad that I got to see Kennedy. I really think I love her. I'm not stupid enough to say it to her though. First, I have to get her to be my official girlfriend. It can't be that hard. I know she already likes me. So here I will make my New Year's resolution. I resolve to be the best boyfriend ever to Kennedy.

I guess I should break up with Anila officially though. I mean, I think we broke up last night, but

I'm not totally sure. She could have just been mad, but if I'm going to be the best boyfriend to Kennedy, I can't have two girlfriends. I'll leave it for a couple of days though. I don't want Anila to yell at me.

Yours truly,
Arthur Bean

▸▸   ▸▸   ▸▸

> Hey, Robbie. I was thinking we could send the camera back in the mail with no return address. No one would ever know where it came from!

no way. that will cost so much $. and it will brake in the mail.

> We can wrap it in a blanket to send it.

dude a stamp costs $1. imagin wat a camera costs to send.

and wat if it got stollen from the mail? that happens all the time. at leest we kno where it is.

Fine. We'll keep it. But one of my resolutions is to not be a criminal. So it's going back.

ya ur such a criminal. its borowwed, not gone 4 eva.

▶▶   ▶▶   ▶▶

Hi, Anila! I wanted to say I'm sorry, but you won't answer your phone! I hope you're doing OK.

I know that NYE didn't play out how you hoped. I'm sorry about that. But I'm not sure that we should be together since we live so far apart. It's too hard when we're not at camp.

Plus, I'm so busy with my movie and school and stuff.

I'm sure that you probably feel sad, but maybe a little relieved too, like me. I hope we can still be friends. ☺

▶▶   ▶▶   ▶▶

I will NEVER feel relieved. Miserable? Heartbroken? Despairing? So very angry that I could literally rip your throat out? These things I feel. But not relieved to be rid of you.

I loved you so much, Arthur. I can't believe you could be such a jerk.

I am really sorry.

Stop it. Just stop.

▸▸   ▸▸   ▸▸

Assignment: Persuasive Writing

Effective persuasive writing can convince your reader of a particular idea, and it's an important skill to practice in essay writing. Write a short essay on one of the following topics, taking a stand on one side of the issue presented. Make sure to choose your arguments effectively and organize your thoughts so that the ideas build on each other. Be sure to provide a counterexample, then try to refute that example with your final example. The topics to choose from:

Would you rather be a vampire or a werewolf? Why?

What is the best superpower to have? Why?

Which is better to watch: television or movies? Why?

Due: January 14

▶▶   ▶▶   ▶▶

ZOMBIE SCHOOL

by Arthur Bean and Robbie Zack and Von Ipo

January 8 Production Meeting Notes

I would like to see a breakdown of scenes for your film and the main action for each. We'll work on this over the next few meetings of the AV Club. Ensure that you make notes of things you'd like to remember in future meetings. —Mrs. Ireland

Scene One: School
In this scene the students are all leaving because there has been an outbreak of zombie at the school. Ms. Whitehead eats a student.

Scene Two: Blazer's House
The GGA trains in a montage. The audience meets the main characters: Blazer, Zipcode, and Tuff Arnold. There are other characters too, like some girlfriends and a few other people in the GGA.

Scene Three: Grocery Store
The GGA runs into ZAP (Zombies Are People) while getting supplies. ZAP is against the GGA.

Scene Four: School
The zombies meet in the basement of the school and make a plan for world dominance.

Scene Five: Blazer's House
The GGA is training. There is a montage.

Scene Six: ZAP Lair
ZAP kidnaps one of the girlfriends of the GGA to use
for information.

Scene Seven: Zipcode's House
Zipcode and Blazer make a secret plan that none of
the GGA know about.

Scene Eight: The Gym
Tuff Arnold works out.

Scene Nine: Around the City
It becomes clear through a montage that the zombie
apocalypse has started.

Scene Ten: ZAP Lair
One of the members of the GGA is seen being a
traitor and joining ZAP.

Scene Eleven: Blazer's House
Zipcode and Blazer tell the GGA about their plan to
make the mall explode and destroy the zombies. We
see the explosions being practiced in a montage. The
traitor (Nunchucks) is there and records the plan so
that ZAP can sabotage it.

Scene Twelve: School
ZAP sends a secret message to the zombies. The
zombies are ready at the mall.

TO BE CONTINUED...

AV CLUB GUIDELINES—Amended #4

1. Any student may join the AV Club.
2. All equipment must be reserved ahead of time and signed out upon use and signed in upon return.
3. Have fun!
4. Filming must take place in sanctioned school areas. There is no filming in areas

restricted to students, such as the basement, the roof, and the staff room.
5. There will be no guns in the film, and other weaponry will be kept to a bare minimum.
6. All equipment must be provided by the students or the drama department. Any additional equipment must be requisitioned through the AV Club administrators.
7. Special effects involving explosions are expressly forbidden.

▸▸   ▸▸   ▸▸

From: Arthur Bean (arthuraaronbean@gmail.com)
To: Kennedy Laurel (imsocutekl@hotmail.com)
Sent: January 8, 19:04

Dear Kennedy,

I thought I should let you know that Anila and I broke up. It was just not the right thing to be together. I think it was pretty mutual.

So if you want to hang out this weekend, I'm always free to see you!

Yours truly,
Arthur Bean

From: Kennedy Laurel (imsocutekl@hotmail.com)
To: Arthur Bean (arthuraaronbean@gmail.com)
Sent: January 8, 22:15

Hi Arthur!

Oh NO! I'm SO sorry to hear about you and Anila! I thought you were such a great couple!
I think that maybe we should not hang out this weekend! I know that when I've been broken up with that I needed some time to be just ME, by myself! Plus, you and I make such great FRIENDS, don't you think?!

Kennedy ☺

From: Arthur Bean (arthuraaronbean@gmail.com)
To: Kennedy Laurel (imsocutekl@hotmail.com)
Sent: January 9, 8:34

Dear Kennedy,

Don't worry about me. I didn't get broken up with! I'm happy to hang out with you anytime doing whatever. It doesn't have to be romantic. Maybe if you're going to the mall or something I could come. Whatever you want to do!

Yours truly,
Arthur Bean

▸▸   ▸▸   ▸▸

Assignment: Persuasive Writing: Television vs. Movies

by Arthur Bean

Everybody wants to be a movie star, but they are in the wrong field. Television is a much better idea. It seems like a crazy idea from someone who is going to be a famous screenwriter. However, my upcoming movie is purely my way to break into the television market. Even Steven Spielberg is making TV shows now!

Television is better if you're an actor or screen-writer, because even though you get smaller pay-checks, you get more of them. For example, my first series will run for over three years. I will negotiate to make over a million dollars per episode. If there are twenty episodes, that's twenty million dollars in one year!

In the TV business, you can also be lazier. Actors on TV shows only have to work an hour a day and only for a few months. In film, the days on a movie set are long and grueling, so you really have to work for your money.

Also, TV is better because more people will know who you are. Even poor people have televisions. So it's easier to be famous and more recognizable around the world.

TV isn't all tea and roses, as my mother would say. As a writer, you need to think about your story arc years in advance. That's a lot more planning than you need to do for a movie.

That's why television is way better than movies,

and I can say that, because I work in movies, so my opinion is pretty balanced.

Arthur,

I appreciate the thought that you put into this assignment. It clearly is a subject that speaks to you. However, be sure to check your facts; a strong argument can be lost when the facts are incorrect. Remember that your conclusion should remind the reader of the arguments you stated in defense of your main point, as well as leave a lasting impression. You don't want to undercut the point you're making by letting the ending go to waste.

Ms. Whitehead

▸▸   ▸▸   ▸▸

DUDE SOS! SOS!!!!

Did someone find out about the camera? Who knows about the camera? Did you tell them that I was only a bystander?

> What are we going to do? I can't leave school or run away. I have a girlfriend! It would break Kennedy's heart if I left.

> I knew this would happen! I told you not to take it! I told you they wouldn't think you were borrowing it. It's in MY closet. What should I do?? Destroy the evidence?!

> NO ITS MY BRO. HES IN JAIL!!!!!!!!!!

> What happened? What did he do? Did he take the fall for the camera?

> Why aren't you responding? I HATE TEXTING!! I'm calling you.

▶▶   ▶▶   ▶▶

January 16th

Dear RJ,

Robbie's brother is a criminal! He got caught shoplifting at the drugstore. They called the cops and everything. Robbie said that his dad had to go down and get Caleb from this little room they have for criminals. It's like a holding cell at the back of the store. I bet it had a two-way mirror. I wonder if they interrogated him like on TV.

Anyway, Robbie is freaked out because the store management is saying that they might press charges. It wasn't even anything really big. He took a couple of packs of mechanical pencils and a thermos. I mean, stealing is stealing, but wouldn't you take something useful? Robbie said that Caleb doesn't seem to care. He said he just went to his room and hasn't come out. Now Robbie isn't allowed to go out, even though he didn't do anything. We'd talked about working on the movie this weekend, but that's not going to happen. Especially because no one can ever see the camera now. At least Robbie finally gets that we can't have the camera around. If his parents or the cops found out, that would be it!

I'll keep you posted about Robbie's brother. Robbie made me promise not to tell anyone, but I don't think you count!

Yours truly,
Arthur Bean

▸▸   ▸▸   ▸▸

From: Von Ipo (thenexteastwood@hotmail.com)
To: Arthur Bean (arthuraaronbean@gmail.com)
Sent: January 18, 17:07

Hey, Arthur!!

How's it going? Did you finish the math homework? I basically got it all done in class, but if you didn't I can help you. I basically can do any math in my head, so it makes it really easy.

I don't have hockey this weekend, so you could come over and I can teach you how to use my video camera. It's pretty detailed, because it's basically top of the line, like what Steven Spielberg uses, but I'm really good at teaching people how to use it. We could even start shooting some of the scenes if you want. I asked Robbie to come too, but he said that he can't but that you didn't have anything to do!

Von

▶▶   ▶▶   ▶▶

> Thanks a lot, man. You really had to tell Von I had nothing to do? I actually have plenty to do. Kennedy and I are hanging out.

> dude no your not I texted w catie last nite and she said she was going to the mall with k.

> Don't believe everything Catie says. She told Ms. Whitehead in class yesterday that Ben had fallen off his roof and broken his back, and all he had was a dentist appointment.

▶▶   ▶▶   ▶▶

January 18th

Dear RJ,

Do you think that Kennedy is actually just going to the mall with Catie? Why wouldn't she invite me to come? I even asked if that was what she was doing, and she never responded.

Do you think that she's mad at me?

I've been racking my brain to think of what I might have done wrong, but I can't come up with anything! I've totally kept my New Year's resolution. I'm pretty sure I've been the best boyfriend ever, even though we're not technically dating. I leave her a note in her locker every day. In one of them I even put a bunch of glitter in the shape of hearts, and I know she opened it, because I saw all the glitter on the floor by her locker on Wednesday. She said that I didn't need to do that, and that it was kind of embarrassing, but I know that she likes the attention.

I tried calling her tonight, but she didn't pick up. I'll try her again in the morning, and maybe she'll invite me then.

Robbie doesn't know what he's talking about. Catie lies about stuff all the time. I don't know why he always talks to her and texts her.

Yours truly,
Arthur Bean

▶▶   ▶▶   ▶▶

Hi, Anila. I just thought I would let you know that there's a show about shark finning that I think you would like.

It's on right now. Channel 17.

Oh man! Sharks are being slaughtered! You should really watch this show! I'm learning so much.

I really am sorry.

▶▶   ▶▶   ▶▶

im SO BORED

I know. Me too.

wat r u doing?

Watching a TV show about animals. Let's have animals in Zombie School! The guinea pigs from the Animal Care Club could be zombies that eat the hamsters.

YES!!! more carnaje the better. did u kno catie started that club?

I bet she never cleans the cages. She just goes to cuddle cute things and then says she's allergic to sawdust.

ive decided im gonna ask catie out

What? WHY?

dude r u kidding? shes hot and shes allways talking 2 me. can u talk 2 kenny and find out if shes single?

I don't really know how to do that.

figger it out.

▶▶   ▶▶   ▶▶

Hey, Artie!

The library is having a giant used-book sale next week. (The sale is giant. Not the books!

At least, I think so!) There's going to be all
kinds of books for sale, and they are still
accepting donations from families. Do you
think you could Dewey decimal me a favor
and write a piece for the <u>Marathon</u>?

Cheers!
Mr. E

▶▶   ▶▶   ▶▶

From: Arthur Bean (arthuraaronbean@gmail.com)
To: Kennedy Laurel (imsocutekl@hotmail.com)
Sent: January 23, 18:10

Dear Kennedy,

I wrote you a poem today when I was bored in science.
I know that sounds so corny, but I wanted you to have it
anyway!

When a boy likes a girl, he buys candy
But in science class, that's not so handy
I wanted to get you some jujubes
But instead, I hope you like these test tubes!

Anyway, I hope you think it's funny. I was thinking that we
could hang out this weekend. I'm happy to do whatever
you want.

Also, do you know if Catie has a boyfriend? I'm just asking for a friend who likes her. IT'S NOT FOR ME!

Yours truly,
Arthur Bean

From: Kennedy Laurel (imsocutekl@hotmail.com)
To: Arthur Bean (arthuraaronbean@gmail.com)
Sent: January 23, 20:04

Hi Arthur!

OMG Does Robbie like Catie?!?! That's HILARIOUS LOL!!! I wonder what she would say if he asks her out! Catie and I are going to the mall this weekend! If you want, you can come with us!
We're going to get perfume samples and maybe go see the new Disney movie LOL! It's going to be SUPER girlie but I think it will be really fun!

Kennedy ☺

From: Arthur Bean (arthuraaronbean@gmail.com)
To: Kennedy Laurel (imsocutekl@hotmail.com)
Sent: January 23, 20:13

Dear Kennedy,

I will be there! What did you think of my poem?
I never said that it was Robbie. I just said a friend. But if it was Robbie, what do you think Catie would say?

Yours truly,
Arthur Bean

▶▶   ▶▶   ▶▶

ZOMBIE SCHOOL

by Arthur Bean and Robbie Zack and Von Ipo

January 24 Production Meeting Notes

Continue working on your scene breakdown. Typical AV Club projects have a running time of seven minutes, as scripts, storyboards, and rehearsal require time and effort. It's better to have a strong short film rather than no film at all. —Mrs. Ireland

Scene Thirteen: The Mall
The GGA meets the zombies, but they are trapped in the food court because the zombies knew about their plans. They kill a lot of zombies, but they lose a lot of the GGA in the battle (they die horrible and gruesome deaths, including Tuff Arnold). Nunchucks is one of the ones who gets killed too, but he apologizes to Blazer as he's going down, and they know that Nunchucks is the one who told the zombies. Blazer and Zipcode have this epic battle with the zombies, and then, when they are cornered, they jump over the McDonald's counter and fight from there. Zipcode notices that there's

another exit out the back, and he yells, "Hey! Blazer! Let's get out of here!" And Blazer yells, "But I'm loving it!!" And Zipcode yells, "Let's go!" So they try and leave, but right as they're getting out the door, a zombie grabs hold of Blazer and rips his arm off. Blazer screams and blacks out, and Zipcode has to grab him and pull him out the door to safety. The last part of the scene is the zombies eating Blazer's arm.

FOR FUTURE MEETINGS:
Tuff Arnold can't die in the mall scene, because I already wrote him into the final scene. —VI

How did YOU write him into the final scene? We don't have a final scene yet. —AB

I started writing outlines so that our script can be awesome! —VI

Actually, Robbie and I are naturals at improv, so we don't need a script. —AB

I thot we were adding ginny pig zombies. —rz

Right! We should put them into the beginning of the movie too. And they can be there, and then die, and come back. Once we're done, let's add that. —AB

like forshadoweing. awesome. —rz

Why are we putting in guinea pig zombies? —VI

It's an inside joke. —AB

Oh, cool! I love inside jokes! —VI

I prefer Von's idea of writing the script to move the filming process along. Projects must be well thought-out and scripted in order to facilitate a successful filming of the project. —Mrs. Ireland

▶▶　　▶▶　　▶▶

AV CLUB GUIDELINES—Amended #5

1. Any student may join the AV Club.
2. All equipment must be reserved ahead of time and signed out upon use and signed in upon return.
3. Have fun!
4. Filming must take place in sanctioned school areas. There is no filming in areas restricted to students, such as the basement, the roof, and the staff room.
5. There will be no guns in the film, and

other weaponry will be kept to a bare minimum.

6. All equipment must be provided by the students or the drama department. Any additional equipment must be requisitioned through the AV Club administrators.
7. Special effects involving explosions are expressly forbidden.
8. Scripts are necessary to facilitate a successful project.

▶▶   ▶▶   ▶▶

Assignment: Introductions and Thesis Statements

Every strong essay has a thesis statement that outlines the writer's overarching point. As we've practiced in class, write an introductory paragraph to a persuasive essay on one of the topics written on the board. You won't be writing the entire essay, but develop your introduction as though you would be. Underline the thesis statement in your paragraph, and outline your three main arguments supporting your thesis statement. Don't forget to hook your audience with a catchy title and unique first sentence!

Due: January 31

▶▶   ▶▶   ▶▶

January 25th

Dear RJ,

I finally get to see Kennedy outside of school tomorrow! It doesn't sound like the most fun thing ever, but at least we'll get to hang out. She's pretty excited to see me.

I think this might be the first time that people who know us will see us hanging out as a couple, basically. I wonder if I should hold her hand. Or should I put my arm on her shoulder? I tried that at New Year's, but I felt so awkward, and I didn't know if I should rest my arm on her shoulders, so I just kind of let it rest lightly, but my arm got really tired like that, so I was glad when she moved. But I see guys practically leaning on their girlfriends. It's like a sign that they are a couple. I want people to see me and Kennedy and think, "Wow. That's a cute couple and they are so in love. Look at how close they stand."

Maybe Catie will like Robbie back, and then the four of us can go out. If Robbie dates Catie, then I bet Robbie and Kennedy will make up and then both Kennedy and Catie could be in our movie and we'll be a powerhouse!

Yours truly,
Arthur Bean

▶▶   ▶▶   ▶▶

January 26th

Dear RJ,

Well, that was the worst mall trip ever. Kennedy wasn't joking about going to get perfume samples. She and Catie walked around this giant makeup store I didn't even know existed—for forty-five minutes—spraying the air in front of them and twirling around in the perfumes. They smelled terrible by the end and I had a headache. Then Kennedy got mad because she asked which perfume I liked best, and I said that I couldn't tell because she had so many on. So then I had to apologize over and over, and I ended up buying all the drinks and candy to sneak into the movie. In case you're wondering, I didn't try putting my arm on her shoulder because I didn't want to smell like all the perfume she had on, so I just walked beside her, trying not to gag.

The worst part was when I tried to ask Catie about Robbie. She thought that I was joking. When I said that I wasn't, she started laughing because she said that it was the funniest thing she'd ever heard. She said she would never go out with him because he was getting so fat and that his brother was a loser. I tried to say that Robbie was really awesome, but she wasn't listening. She was just making jokes with Kennedy about how Robbie would take her out for dinner, but she would have to eat beforehand because he would probably eat her meal too.

It was terrible. Kennedy was laughing too and I didn't know what to say, so I didn't say anything. I just fake laughed because I didn't want them to think I was a loser too. I felt so bad for doing it, especially because Robbie isn't that fat and I don't think he's a loser, but his brother is a loser, so some of Catie's jokes were actually pretty funny.

But now I don't know what to tell Robbie when he asks about what Catie said. Maybe I should tell him that Latha likes him, and then he'll forget about Catie. Man, RJ. I thought only girls had to deal with this kind of stuff!

Yours truly,
Arthur Bean

▶▶   ▶▶   ▶▶

did catie ask about me at the mall? wat did she say?

> I didn't ask her. I don't think you should ask her out.

im going to do it.

> I really don't think you should ask Catie out. She's best friends with Kennedy. You hate Kennedy. If you date Catie, you would have to hang out with Kennedy too, you know.

too late. i texted her and asked her out. fingers xed!

▶▶ ▶▶ ▶▶

Book It to This Sale!

by Arthur Bean

The library is hosting a used-book sale the size of *War and Peace* this week, and it's going to be as epic as *The Odyssey*! There will be a huge number of discarded library books, both fiction and nonfiction, so if you are in the market for a set of *Encyclopedia Britannica* from 1987, get there early! These books will be flying off the shelves because of the low, low prices. There are some great books being sold, plus new stuff being put out every day, so come back more than once.

A number of parents have also donated books, so get here early to reclaim your well-loved books that your parents thought you wouldn't notice were gone. Trust me, if you don't have a full, perfect set of Harry Potter when you're eighty, you're going to be so mad at your younger self!

All proceeds from the used-book sale will go into buying better books for the library, so it's a great cause, because maybe this way they will replace the class set of *Hamlet* with *Diary of a Wimpy Kid*!

What's the best part about buying books at the used-book sale at the library? There's no way you can overdue it!

The sale runs Wednesday to Friday, at lunchtime, and again from 3:30 until 6:00 p.m.

Hey, Artie!

This is great! I like how you used appropriate humor but also remained positive about the sale. I'm sure the books will fly off the shelves. Here's hoping they raise enough money to add stories to the school building. Get it? Stories?

Mr. E

⏩   ⏩   ⏩

From: Kennedy Laurel (imsocutekl@hotmail.com)
To: Arthur Bean (arthuraaronbean@gmail.com)
Sent: January 29, 18:58

Hi Arthur!

Did you hear about Robbie asking Catie out?!?! LOL!! I can't believe he did it!! Catie called me when she got his text and she was KILLING HERSELF laughing! Catie showed all our friends at lunch today, and it was pretty funny LOL! He even attached a bathroom mirror selfie of him wearing his dad's tie or something and holding a construction paper heart. It's so weird! I NEVER thought Robbie would try and be romantic LOL!

    I ALMOST feel bad for him, he looks so dumb in the picture!

I'm glad you've never tried to do anything like that! You have good taste LOL!

Kennedy ☺

From: Arthur Bean (arthuraaronbean@gmail.com)
To: Kennedy Laurel (imsocutekl@hotmail.com)
Sent: January 29, 19:17

Dear Kennedy,

I swear I had nothing to do with Robbie!! I tried to tell him not to ask her out, but he really likes her.

Robbie's mom is coming back to Calgary this weekend, which means that I've got lots of time to hang out! We were supposed to work on the movie script without Von and Mrs. Ireland getting in the way. (She is driving me crazy. Does she have a thousand rules for class too?) I'll probably still work on it, but I want to see you! We never get to hang out just you and me! Do you want to come for pizza on Saturday night? After dinner, we can watch a movie or something, just you and me. Your choice of movie, of course! ☺

Yours truly,
Arthur Bean

PS: Did you get the notes I left in your locker today? I tried to fold them into origami flowers, but I couldn't get them in, so they probably looked messy, but don't think that's a reflection on you!

▶▶   ▶▶   ▶▶

> know wat sux? mom is pressing her custoddy case cuz calebs a dumass.

> What?? What do you mean? Did she come here to take you with her? To North Carolina? She can't do that! You're not even an American!

> IM NOT GOING. LET CALEB GO TO JAIL.

▶▶   ▶▶   ▶▶

January 30th

Dear RJ,

I just got off the phone with Robbie. His mom flew back here because she thinks that Robbie's dad is being a terrible dad and she thinks that Caleb and Robbie should move to North Carolina with her. All because Caleb stole mechanical pencils. And what about the stupid video camera in my closet? If Robbie's mom finds out about the camera, then he'll definitely have to move. He knows it too. That's probably why he's talking about Caleb so much. But I can't take the fall for it. I was barely involved! Also, we didn't really steal it on purpose. We just wanted to borrow it. And it's not exactly the same as stealing from a big store like Caleb did. I don't know why he stole that stuff. At least we needed the camera!

It's not fair! Robbie can't move. If he left, I'd have to rewrite the whole movie by myself. Or worse, with Von. And if Robbie moves, who would I hang out with on the weekends? I can only take so much perfume sampling with Kennedy and her friends. It would just be me and Pickles again, hanging out at home. Stupid cat.

Yours truly,
Arthur Bean

FEBRUARY

Assignment: Don't You Carrot All?

by Arthur Bean

It's all over the television and debated heavily by parents: Should there only be healthy options in the Terry Fox Junior High cafeteria? The movement to ban junk food is gaining momentum, but there is another side to this story. So far, no one has asked the students what they want. <u>This essay will show why it's important that junk food remain an option in the school cafeteria.</u> There are many arguments as to why, but this essay will explore three major points supporting this argument. Students need to be given the freedom and experience to make good choices. Science has shown that if you eat junk food, you get fat. Well, if students don't want to get fat, maybe they need to learn the hard way. Or maybe they have a good metabolism and can eat whatever they want. Also, junk food is a treat that students shouldn't be denied at school. For many kids, school is hard enough, and then to only get lentil soup or celery sticks at lunch? That would suck. And the last point explored in this essay is that removing junk food severely limits the number of puns that can be made. How, I ask you, will we still have Fry-Day if there are no fries allowed?

Arthur,

This is nicely done. Your introduction is concise and engaging and covers all the necessary material. Two of your three points have some real weight to them; however, your secondary remarks weaken your argument.

Should you use this topic in the final in-class essay assignment, focus on strengthening your stance with facts rather than judgment. You should also think about a stronger third topic; food puns will not carry a lot of weight here. And please pay better attention to the assignment due dates.

Ms. Whitehead

Ms. Whitehead,

I think you are missing the power of the written word here. Lettuce be clear, most kids in the school donut understand a good pun, but if we keep trying to taco bout it, they will ketchup.

Yours truly,
Arthur Bean

catie rote back!

Took her long enough. What did she say?

that I am sweet. lol. she cleerly doesnt kno me.

That's all? Did she say that she would go out with you?

i think that text speaks for itsself

I don't. I think you should ask for a real answer.

whatever dude. k doesnt even hang out with u. i dont think u can give realation ship advice.

From: Arthur Bean (arthuraaronbean@gmail.com)
To: Kennedy Laurel (imsocutekl@hotmail.com)
Sent: February 3, 12:07

Dear Kennedy,

I was thinking about you this weekend! I think that enough time has passed since Anila and I broke up that I'm ready to date someone else. And I'm really thinking that that person should be you! After all, we have such great chemistry and I know we already like each other.
What do you think?

Yours truly,
Arthur Bean

From: Kennedy Laurel (imsocutekl@hotmail.com)
To: Arthur Bean (arthuraaronbean@gmail.com)
Sent: February 3, 15:56

Hi Arthur!

That's really sweet! You're always so sweet! But I REALLY think that I was feeling confused when I said I liked you! I got all mixed up and maybe I shouldn't have said anything! I really like having you as my friend! I don't want to RUIN that!
I know that it probably seems SO MEAN to you! But Catie and Jill and I were talking about it, and Catie says that I need to tell it to you straight! So don't hate me, OK?!

Kennedy ☺

▸▸   ▸▸   ▸▸

February 3rd

Dear RJ,

Valentine's Day is coming up, so I need to do something really big and romantic for Kennedy. Maybe Luke will have an idea. He always has good ideas.

I love Kennedy, but I didn't know that dating her was going to be this hard! I just need her to say that she is mine. I'm sure that it's just that Catie is telling her lies about me. All Catie cares about is what other people think. But once I can convince Kennedy that I'm one hundred percent hers, I'm sure things will get better and it'll be more relaxing soon. I hope so. I'm running out of words that rhyme with love! (Just kidding. I ran out of words that rhyme with love after my first poem!)

Yours truly,
Arthur Bean

▶▶   ▶▶   ▶▶

Assignment: The Gratitude Project

We often think of Valentine's Day as being a day for romantic love, but the Gratitude Project asks us to think of it as something more. This is a great opportunity to thank someone you love for the qualities they bring to you. You can use any form of writing that you prefer. Some of you may want to write a letter, a poem, a comic strip, even a short story highlighting some of the qualities that you love about a person and saying thank you for what positive things he or she has brought to your life. Speak from the heart!

Due: February 14

▶▶   ▶▶   ▶▶

From: Arthur Bean (arthuraaronbean@gmail.com)
To: Kennedy Laurel (imsocutekl@hotmail.com)
Sent: February 6, 20:10

Dear Kennedy,

I wanted to cordially invite you to come to the Valentine's Day Dance with me next Thursday. Will you be my date? I'll buy your ticket!
    Of course, we'd be going as friends. I totally understand that you don't want to ruin that. So, let's not ruin it, and let me buy your ticket to the dance!

Yours truly,
Arthur Bean

From: Kennedy Laurel (imsocutekl@hotmail.com)
To: Arthur Bean (arthuraaronbean@gmail.com)
Sent: February 6, 21:39

Hi Arthur!

Aw! That's so so sweet!

I already PROMISED Catie and Jill that I would hang out with them at the dance! GIRL POWER LOL!!

Kennedy ☺

From: Arthur Bean (arthuraaronbean@gmail.com)
To: Kennedy Laurel (imsocutekl@hotmail.com)
Sent: February 6, 21:43

Dear Kennedy,

That's great that you're going! We can hang out there all together. We'll dance the night away. Anila said that I'm a pretty good dancer, so hopefully you think so too! I don't have a ride there, so do you think your mom or dad could pick me up?

Yours truly,
Arthur Bean

▶▶   ▶▶   ▶▶

ZOMBIE SCHOOL

by Robbie Zack and Arthur Bean and Von Ipo

February 7 Production Meeting Notes

It is imperative that you remember that this is a

school and a learning institution. Ensure that your film's content remains suitable for children as you finish the storyboard notes. —Mrs. Ireland

Scene Fourteen: The Hospital
Blazer gets a new bionic arm.

Scene Fifteen: ZAP Lair
The zombies descend on the ZAP lair and kill them all, proving them wrong.

Scene Sixteen: The Hospital
Blazer is testing out his new arm when he looks out the window and sees the ZAP lair blow up. He rips out all the tubes and IVs and runs out of the hospital.

Scene Seventeen: The Sewer
Tuff Arnold emerges from the sewer, where he was hiding to gather information about ZAP. He runs from the blast.

Scene Eighteen: Zipcode's House
Zipcode sees the blast too and starts stockpiling weapons. While he's doing that, Blazer busts through the door and Zipcode says, without even looking up, "Took you long enough." Blazer says, "It's snowing. Slowed me down." Zipcode says, "I thought you were ready for that." Blazer says, "I am." And then his bionic arm becomes a shovel. He says, "I could get here, but it was tricky just to get a coat on." Zipcode says, "A blazer?" Blazer punches him and says, "If you're not careful, I'll shove you in a mailbox and see where you end up, Zipcode!"

TO REMEMBER:
We need to talk to a surgeon about how a bionic arm works. —AB

Or an FX guy. my arm needs a shovel, a gun, a grenade lawncher, chopstix, and a reglar hand. —rz

You should already have the regular hand. —AB

watch it. my hand is superstrength and it can strangle u like a python. —rz

I'll talk to the city to find out how to get into the sewers. My mom knows the mayor, so it won't be a problem for me to get in there. —VI

Be careful. There could be pythons down there. It would be really, really sad if you were killed making the movie. We would be sooooo lost. —AB

Don't worry! I can find a machete to bring. That would be good in the zombie scenes too! —VI

Please refer back to Point 5 in the AV Club policy:

5. There will be no guns in the film, and other weaponry will be kept to a bare minimum.

And make note of this addition:

8. Scripts are necessary to facilitate a successful project.

⏩   ⏩   ⏩

February 10th

Dear RJ,

I hung out at Robbie's today. His parents have started actual, legal divorce proceedings and his mom wants full-time custody. Robbie said that she says that all boys fail at life without their mother.

That makes me really mad, because some of us don't get a choice! I mean, my dad isn't awesome all the time, and we don't talk a lot, but I don't think he's doing a bad job because my mom's gone. I'm not failing at life! I don't know her at all, but I hate Mrs. Zack. Maybe if she hadn't left her family behind, Caleb would be fine. Robbie said that she can't force him to go to the States though. They have to stay in the same province, so she has to choose between her boyfriend or her kids. Since she chose her boyfriend before, I bet she doesn't follow through.

Still, it sucks for Robbie.

Yours truly,
Arthur Bean

▶▶   ▶▶   ▶▶

From: Arthur Bean (arthuraaronbean@gmail.com)
To: Kennedy Laurel (imsocutekl@hotmail.com)
Sent: February 11, 22:43

Dear Kennedy,

Did you get my email about getting a ride with you to the dance? My dad has a yoga thing, so he can't take me. I can be ready whenever! Let me know what time, and I'll be waiting.

Yours truly,
Arthur Bean

▶▶   ▶▶   ▶▶

Do you know if Catie is going to the dance with Kennedy? I need a ride.

dunno. if she is tho, u better not dance w/her!!! She's mine!

Yeah. That's not going to be a problem. I wish you'd come.

not my thing dude. im thinking i should take the camera and record the fites b/w my mom, dad, and bro. its reality show worthy. then i could make millions and divorce them instead.

▶▶   ▶▶   ▶▶

February 14th

Dear RJ,

This sucks. I can't believe that my dad would go to his stupid yoga thing and not make sure I had a ride to the dance. I can't believe Catie, who ignored me at school today when I asked for a ride. She's awful. I saw Robbie talking to her, and then as soon as he left, she turned to her friends and was clearly making fun of him. They were all laughing. I couldn't hear what they were saying, but I know it was probably mean.

I've tried to tell Robbie that Catie isn't nice, but he shuts me down. I'm mad at Kennedy because she never emailed or called me back about getting a ride. And I'm mad at Nicole for choosing the worst week to go away. While I'm at it, I'm mad at Ms. Whitehead for giving us a stupid homework assignment and I'm mad at Mrs. Ireland for ruining the movie and I'm mad at Von because he's so annoying and I'm mad at Luke because he doesn't live here!

I'm just going to take the bus to the dance. I don't care. Dad said that he could pick me up, so I'm going to leave a note for him to pick me up, and I'm going to go. It's not quite a steed, but I'm going to be Kennedy's prince tonight!

Yours truly,
Arthur Bean

▶▶   ▶▶   ▶▶

February 14th

Dear RJ,

I never should have gone to that STUPID DANCE!! I HAVE NEVER BEEN SO MAD EVER!!!!!!!

Yours truly,
Arthur Bean

February 15th

Dear RJ,

Sometimes a personal day comes at exactly the right time. Like today. I spent the whole morning by myself watching TV and working on the end of the zombie movie, and I think that now I'm ready to tell you about the dance last night.

I took the bus there, and it took me forever. By the time I got there, I thought it would have started already, but there weren't very many people yet and I didn't want to go in alone. So I walked around the school, trying to see in the gym without anyone seeing that I was there, and I kind of watched people going in, to see when Kennedy arrived and then pretend that I had just gotten there at the same time. But then Von came up and he was talking to me about the movie and all this stupid stuff, and I missed seeing Kennedy. I had to push past him to get to the dance, and when I got in the gym, Kennedy and Catie and Jill were dancing already. I tried to get Kennedy's attention, but every time I came up to them, Catie would turn to block Kennedy from me.

I tried a few times to join them, but Catie just kept making sure that I was dancing by myself, and Kennedy didn't stop her. I finally stopped trying to talk to her at all, and then SANDY—stupid, dumb Sandy who went out with Kennedy last year—came over and I watched the two of them talking and dancing and laughing with a whole bunch of people. I felt like a tiny bug on the sidewalk. I half wanted to leave, but I also didn't want to leave in case she came over to find me. Then the DJ said that there was one more song before the last song, and Kennedy and her friends all left the dance. I thought they were just going to the bathroom, but then they didn't come back. I just stood there watching the door, with stupid Von beside me talking nonstop. And then the dance was over, and my dad was late picking me up, so I was the last one there and I had to help take down all the decorations and wash the dishes that were left over.

I've never felt more stupid, RJ. I don't even know what to say to Kennedy. Do I talk to her? Why would she let Catie do that?

Yours truly,
Arthur Bean

▶▶   ▶▶   ▶▶

Arthur,

I haven't received your last English assignment on gratitude. This is the second assignment in a row that has been tardy. Please feel free to talk to me if there is anything going on at home that is prohibiting

you from submitting assignments on time.
This kind of forgetfulness is not like you!

Ms. Whitehead

▶▶   ▶▶   ▶▶

Assignment: Thanks, Pickles

by Arthur Bean

Dear Pickles,

You are a demon cat, but thank you for sticking around, even after Mom died. I know you don't like me or Dad very much, but you hang around anyway. You've taught me a lot of things too. You taught me that sometimes you need to draw blood to get the attention that you want. You taught me that it's OK to hide when you don't want to see people and that they (mostly) will still be there when you come back. You taught me that sometimes you have to act like someone totally different than who you are to get what you want. I've seen you be really nice to Nicole because she sometimes gives you bits of canned tuna or little nibbles of cheese. So thanks for kind of being there sometimes, Pickles.

Since you can't read English, here's a recap: Meow meow mew. Meow, mew, meowwww. Meeee ooooow-www. Meow.

Arthur,

I'm uncertain as to why you chose your cat to thank. The point of this assignment was not to be humorous, but to reflect upon those who have made a lasting impression and thank them. I believe that you could have tried a lot harder. I know you're a strong writer, Arthur, and your reflections are often much more in-depth. This is just not up to your usual quality.

Again, if there is any problem you wish to discuss with me, please see me. My door is always open.

Ms. Whitehead

▶▶   ▶▶   ▶▶

ZOMBIE SCHOOL

by Arthur Bean and Robbie Zack and Von Ipo

February 21 Production Meeting Notes

I'm concerned that your ideas have gotten out of control. Should you expect to film any of your movie, the storyboard outline must be completed today. Do not exceed twenty scenes in your planning. —Mrs. Ireland

Scene Nineteen: Zipcode's Secret Weapons Lair
Tuff Arnold arrives and Zipcode and Blazer have gotten together the last remaining soldiers from the GGA. They all prepare for a final battle against the zombies, who have left every other city and descended upon Calgary because they heard that the GGA was the most powerful army in the world, and to achieve full zombie world domination, they have to kill them off. There is really powerful music playing in this scene, like maybe heavy rap music.

Scene Twenty: School
The zombies from around North America are preparing for battle too, in a montage.

Scene Twenty-One: School Gym
The GGA lures all the zombies into the school gym and locks the doors. Then they attack from the storage room, throwing all the balls and equipment at the zombies. The zombies are losing limbs left and right! Most of the GGA is also killed by zombies. In the end, there are only Tuff Arnold and Zipcode and Blazer left. They are surrounded by zombies, and it looks like they're going to die. But then Blazer looks at Zipcode, and says, "It's time," and he points to his bionic wrist. On the wrist where there would be a watch is a self-destruct button. Zipcode says, "No way, man. You don't have to do that." Blazer says, "I do." Tuff Arnold says, "Do what?" Zipcode ignores him, and says, "Take us with you." Blazer says, "No. You have to rebuild the world. Make a zombie-free world. For the children." Tuff Arnold says, "What are you planning to do?!" Zipcode says, "Then at least

take Tuff Arnold with you." Blazer pushes Zipcode and Tuff away. "Go. Now." They hesitate, but the zombies are getting really close. "RUN!" Zipcode and Tuff run away, and leave Blazer in the gym.

Scene Twenty-Two: Outside the School
As Zipcode and Tuff Arnold run out the doors, the school blows up. It is snowing lightly outside. Tuff Arnold mutters, "I guess school's out...forever." Zipcode takes off his blazer and holds it up to the sky. "You did it, man. You're a hero." Music swells as the sun sets over the blazer, and Zipcode is still standing, lit by the fire of the school in the background. Blackout. Credits roll.

NOTES FOR LATER:
I like that my caracter blows up the school. —rz

I'm really great at chemistry. I had a chemistry set growing up and can do awesome stuff to make it all really real. —VI

I think we need city permits to blow up buildings. I can forge my dad's signature on them. —AB

Please refer back to Points 5, 6, and 7 in the AV Club policy. And my note about a maximum number of twenty scenes in your script. —Mrs. Ireland

  5. There will be no guns in the film, and other weaponry will be kept to a bare minimum.
  6. Special effects involving explosions are expressly forbidden.
  7. Scripts are necessary to facilitate a successful project.

▶▶   ▶▶   ▶▶

From: Kennedy Laurel (imsocutekl@hotmail.com)
To: Arthur Bean (arthuraaronbean@gmail.com)
Sent: February 22, 17:02

Hi Arthur!

How are you? I haven't heard from you in AGES! Are you mad at me?!

   I feel like you might be mad at me because Catie thought she was being funny at the dance! She really wanted it to be a girls' night though! I hope you aren't angry! I really do want us to be friends!

Kennedy ☹

From: Arthur Bean (arthuraaronbean@gmail.com)
To: Kennedy Laurel (imsocutekl@hotmail.com)
Sent: February 22, 21:00

Dear Kennedy,

Of course I'm not mad at you. I've been really busy with the movie and writing. Plus, we've had so much homework. It's almost as though the teachers think that because it's cold out, we have all this time to do whatever we want.

What are you doing this weekend? I'm always free to hang out. Just say the word and I'll be there! We can do anything. I hear that they have free public skating on Sundays evenings at the community center. I could take you skating. It would be like a belated Valentine's Day activity!

Yours truly,
Arthur Bean

From: Kennedy Laurel (imsocutekl@hotmail.com)
To: Arthur Bean (arthuraaronbean@gmail.com)
Sent: February 23, 11:07

Hi Arthur!

Oh phew!! I was worried there LOL!

I can't go skating this weekend, but thanks for asking! I know what you mean about the homework! I'm so swamped with school stuff! I promised Catie I would be her partner for the science fair, but somehow, every time we meet, we never get as much done as we think we will.

I'm SURE it's not because we start talking about other stuff LOL! Anyway, we are getting together all weekend to work on our project and this time we will finish it. (Probably not!) We're doing ours on calories and what they mean and stuff! It means we get to test lots of junk food LOL!

I also hope you're joking about the Valentine's Day activity! FRIENDS don't do Valentine's Day stuff!!

Kennedy ☺

From: Arthur Bean (arthuraaronbean@gmail.com)
To: Kennedy Laurel (imsocutekl@hotmail.com)
Sent: February 23, 12:46

Dear Kennedy,

Of course I was joking! You should hang around with me more. You're starting to not recognize my witty jokes! We'll have to hang out next weekend. Good luck with your science project!

Yours truly,
Arthur Bean

▶▶   ▶▶   ▶▶

February 23rd

Dear RJ,

I'm not mad at Kennedy anymore. I was for a while, but how can I stay mad at her? She seemed really upset in her email and I don't want to upset her. She's so worried that we won't be friends anymore if we date, but I'm pretty sure that a lot of couples are still friends when they are together.

My parents always said that they were each other's best friend, so Kennedy just needs to hear stuff like that and she'll come around. I invited her to do the most romantic thing ever, so maybe next week we can skate. We'll hold hands and then she'll start to fall, and I'll have to try and catch her, but I won't do a very good job, and I'll fall first and then she'll fall on top of me and we'll make out.

Yours truly,
Arthur Bean

▸▸   ▸▸   ▸▸

Hey, Artie,

Have I got a sweet article for you! The ninth-grade home ec final baking project is a bake sale, and I know you've got a sweet tooth. Could you do a write-up about the delicious sweets these students have made? Please remember to be kind; the home ec class has worked hard to perfect their treats. I want you to use your good ol' Artie charm *and not serve up your finely honed critique methods for this assignment!*

Cheers!
Mr. E

▶▶   ▶▶   ▶▶

Assignment: Judge a Book by Its Cover

We're starting our novel study unit, and due to popular demand, you'll have a choice of novels to work on! Please choose one of the following three novels:

The Dark Is Rising by Susan Cooper
Invitation to the Game by Monica Hughes
Kensuke's Kingdom by Michael Morpurgo

Examine the cover of the book you chose, and answer the following questions in a short paragraph:

Why did you pick that particular book versus the other two?
What does the cover tell you?
What do you think the story will be like?
What are you expecting to happen in the book?

Due: March 5

MARCH

March 3rd

Dear RJ,

Most boring weekend ever. Robbie was mooning over Catie the whole time we hung out. I don't know why he bothers. He texts her and asks her to do stuff, but she always tells him she's busy. He should just give it up already.

I got so bored watching him on his phone that I even texted Anila to say hello, but she never texted me back. I don't blame her, really, although I'm trying to be a good guy. I mean, what if we both go to camp next year and have to see each other?

I kind of miss talking to her. I told her stuff that I never told anyone (except you, RJ). And she just listened to me, and sometimes she gave me advice, but not always. That was pretty nice.

Yours truly,
Arthur Bean

▸▸   ▸▸   ▸▸

mom says we r going to nc for spring break. dad says over his dead body. my bros a criminnal and my mom is about to be a murderer. my family is crazy

Can you tell her you need to be here? We need to film the movie over spring break! How else are we going to get to put blood all over the school?

You can stay with us if you have to. My dad won't even notice that you're here, I bet.

▶▶   ▶▶   ▶▶

Assignment: *The Dark Is Rising* Book Cover

by Arthur Bean

I picked *The Dark Is Rising* by Susan Cooper because I've read it at least four times before. This way, I don't have to read it again. I think everyone should have chosen *The Dark Is Rising* because it's one of the best books ever written. Whenever I read it, I wish I had written it. Looking at the cover, I think it would be mostly about wild horses, because the horse on the cover looks crazy and like he's going to attack the boy cowering underneath him.

I would also assume that it takes place in the summer, because the guy doesn't have a jacket on. But I know that it takes place around Christmas. I think the story will be very mysterious and dark, with twinges of King Arthur legends in it. I think that this book will make me want to stay up all night reading, underneath thick covers with a mug of hot chocolate when it's snowing outside.

Arthur,

I'm glad that you enjoyed reading <u>The Dark Is Rising</u> so much. It's one of my favorites too. But since you're already so familiar with the book, please choose another of the novels, so that you can approach the book fresh and then see if your expectations have been met. That is the point of this exercise.

Ms. Whitehead

▶▶   ▶▶   ▶▶

ZOMBIE SCHOOL

by Arthur Bean, Robbie Zack and Von Ipo

March 7 Production Meeting Notes

Gentlemen, I have strong reservations about your storyboards and script notes; as we progress, I expect that you will be fully cooperative in the editing process. However, to remain on schedule, please look at how you would like to cast your film, keeping in mind that every student interested must be given equal opportunity in the selection process. I trust that there will be no nepotism in the audition process. —Mrs. Ireland

since we don't know what neppottism means, I dout there will be any of that hapening were just going to choose people we like anyway. —rz

Do you guys want me to write up some audition monologues? I've already got this awesome one where one girl is actually Tuff Arnold's sister, Muffy Arnold, and she sees her long-lost brother after twenty years of living apart. —VI

lets use parts of the walking dead show as audition peaces. that show is awesome! —rz

We could use that one, and maybe some of *Shaun of the Dead*, because everyone in that one is British, so we can see if people can do accents. —AB

we need 1 with lots of swearing so we kno people sound natural when they are killing zombies. —rz

Please note item 1 and a new item 9 of the AV Club policy. —Mrs. Ireland

1. Any student may join the AV Club.
9. Language in the script and on set must be appropriate for all ages.

▸▸   ▸▸   ▸▸

Assignment: Tweet Your Book Review!

As you work through our novel study, write four tweets about the novel you have chosen. Focus on keeping information about your experience reading the book brief but engaging; tweets can only be 140 characters, including letters, spaces, and punctuation. Use your words wisely; the best novel responses will be featured on the school's public Twitter account!

Due: March 22

▸▸   ▸▸   ▸▸

Sweet Treats and Gooey Eats

by Arthur Bean

Calling all dentists! This is your chance to get some new patients, because there's no way the students at Terry Fox Junior High were able to resist the gourmet delights of the ninth-grade home ec class. As the final exam for their baking unit, Mrs. Chao's classes got to choose their own recipes, and a friendly competition was waged at the bake sale.

The first treats to go were, surprisingly, those of Sandy Dickason and Victor Hsiao. I never tried them because I don't trust Sandy at all, but their chocolate chili cake slices seemed to be a hit. A close second were the coconut macaroons; everyone raved about their sweet centers. I tried the snickerdoodles, which were the perfect blend of crunchy and chewy, the caramel blondies, which would have been better if there hadn't been actual blond hair in them, and the chocolate fudge drops, which were pretty good too. Everything was sold out by the end of the day on Wednesday, except for a few Rice Krispies squares. It marked a very successful bake sale, although it was decidedly less fun for those taking the bus home with Connor "Pukey" Tooey.

Oh, Artie,

It's actually impressive that you are consistently able to write articles that are simultaneously celebratory and defamatory. You've really been improving, but again, I'll be doing some edits to tone down your editorial voice. Come by after school to chat about what you need to work on in order to continue improving your articles.

Mr. E

Dear Mr. Everett,

I really think that you're missing the point of
my articles. If I had my own column, readers
would better understand my witty sense of
humor. It seems to be lost on a lot of people
these days, but Robbie Zack said that I'm
like olives. Even if you hate olives, if you keep
tasting one every day, you'll eventually really
like them. Maybe you'll even crave them. Think
about it.

Yours truly,
Arthur Bean

Artie,

I need to see you grow as a reporter and be
objective in your articles before you'll have
your own column. You need to be able to
report on "olive" the story, not just make a
joke of it!

Mr. E

▶▶   ▶▶   ▶▶

CALL NOTICE FOR ZOMBIE MOVIE!!!

**Be in the greatest movie ever made
at Terry Fox Junior High!**

NO EXPERIENCE NECESSARY
(but is recommended)

**SIGN UP TO AUDITION AT
THE DRAMA ROOM**

**AUDITIONS ARE MARCH 20 and 21
AFTER SCHOOL**

GET FAMOUS!

**TALK TO ARTHUR BEAN
OR ROBBIE ZACK (in homeroom 8B)
FOR INFORMATION!!**
* or Von Ipo *

(Teachers are also welcome!)

▶▶   ▶▶   ▶▶

> We have to get the camera back before spring break. I can't handle it anymore!

why r u handling it? I thot we agreed not to touch it hahaha

> It's not funny, Robbie! My dad saw it today and started asking a bunch of questions.

> I had to say that Mrs. Ireland lent it to me and he said that it was odd that the school would lend out such a nice piece of electronic equipment. He's onto us!!

k fine. well talk bout it this w-end and come up w/a plan. but AFTER tryouts.

▶▶   ▶▶   ▶▶

March 16th

Dear RJ,

Robbie and I tried to come up with a plan to get the stupid camera back, but we came up with nothing! It's impossible. There's no way that we can get to camp without it being really suspicious. The best we did was telling my dad that there was a bottle drive for school and saying that there were lots of bottles out on the highway near camp and that we could stop in to say hi to Tomasz and Halina and get their bottles too, but he said that we could take the ones from the apartment building's recycling room. Robbie said that he wouldn't go garbage picking anyway.

Now I still have the camera, and my dad keeps bringing it up in conversation. I don't know why he's so interested in the camera. He keeps asking about the movie and how it's going and how the camera works and how long I'm allowed to keep it. He's never shown interest in anything else at school before. I can't keep lying to him. Well, actually, I can. I just don't want to. Maybe I can hide it at Nicole's apartment. Her place is so full of stuff that she'd never find it at the bottom of her wool stash!

Yours truly,
Arthur Bean

▸▸   ▸▸   ▸▸

From: Arthur Bean (arthuraaronbean@gmail.com)
To: Kennedy Laurel (imsocutekl@hotmail.com)
Sent: March 17, 9:22

Dear Kennedy,

Happy Saint Patrick's Day! I heard you telling Catie that your mom is from Ireland, so are you guys celebrating today? Do you eat a lot of potatoes and watch movies with Sean Connery in them?

Maybe I could take you for a green milk shake at Peter's. I think they are mint flavored, but they could be lime. You don't even need to have a green milk shake. You could have any flavor you want! If you don't think that you can finish one by yourself, I don't mind sharing a milk shake with you.

Let me know!

Yours truly,
Arthur Bean

From: Kennedy Laurel (imsocutekl@hotmail.com)
To: Arthur Bean (arthuraaronbean@gmail.com)
Sent: March 17, 13:41

Hi Arthur!

Thanks for the invitation, but I'm busy today! Have a good rest of your weekend though!

Kennedy ☺

▶▶   ▶▶   ▶▶

March 19th

Dear RJ,

Auditions are tomorrow! I can't wait to see the lines down the hall for people who want a part. I bet we'll be there for hours. Today we set up a table with water bottles on it and copies of the audition scripts. I've been practicing my stone face so that people auditioning don't know what I'm thinking. It's really important. I don't want girls to start crying because they think that they didn't get the part. I snuck the camera out yesterday, so it's in my locker now. Hopefully I can leave it there from now on.

I hope we get talented people to audition—and lots of teachers. We wrote a juicy part for Ms. Whitehead. She better be good enough to play that part.

Yours truly,
Arthur Bean

▸▸   ▸▸   ▸▸

March 21st

Dear RJ,

I can't believe it! No one came to our auditions! Not even Kennedy, and I was sure she would come. She said a long time ago that she was going to be in our movie! Instead, Robbie and I had to sit there with Von, waiting for people. Robbie drew some good examples for the gore makeup we need, which was the only good thing from today. Von just kept talking and saying stuff like how people would have come if they knew he was involved, but that he didn't tell anyone because he didn't want to be mobbed. I thought maybe everyone was waiting until the second day to audition because they wanted to be memorable, but then today no one showed up either. How can we have crowd scenes and armies if there are only three people in the movie? Robbie said that he didn't really care and that he kind of liked Von's idea of making it an animated movie using Robbie's illustrations, but then I get left out entirely. And it was basically my idea to start with. I'm the brains behind this whole thing! Plus, I doubt that Von actually knows how to animate stuff. I don't believe anything he says.

Yours truly,
Arthur Bean

▶▶   ▶▶   ▶▶

Assignment: Tweet Your Book Review

by Arthur Bean

Twitter Feed for *Invitation to the Game* by Monica Hughes

I hope the "game" they want to play is a version

of *The Hunger Games*, and that the hippie weirdo Scylla is the first to go. She's too perky.

The game is totally opposite from *The Hunger Games*. They can't die! If only this existed last year. My whole family would have played.

I'm pretty sure I could win the game with just me, Robbie, and Luke. No need for Scylla & her hippie ways, or Rich's complaining. He's the worst.

Invitation to the Game was pretty good, even though no one died (SPOILER ALERT!). Though why would anyone marry Scylla?

Arthur,

These are excellent tweets about your reading experience. I'm glad you enjoyed the novel, except for the character of Scylla. It's interesting that you had such a strong reaction to such a minor character. I've always enjoyed Monica Hughes's books, and I hope that our novel study has inspired you to read more of her work. I know you enjoy science fiction and dystopian novels; if you'd like suggestions for some books similar to Hughes's, feel free to come chat!

Ms. Whitehead

▶▶   ▶▶   ▶▶

CALL NOTICE FOR ZOMBIE MOVIE!!!

**Be in the greatest movie ever made at
Terry Fox Junior High!**

PLENTY OF ROLES for teachers!

EVEN MORE for students!

NO EXPERIENCE NECESSARY

NO AUDITION NECESSARY!!!!

3:30 APRIL 4 AT THE DRAMA ROOM

▶▶   ▶▶   ▶▶

Assignment: Personal Novel Study

Choose a novel, either from the school library or from our class-room shelves, that you think you will enjoy reading over spring break. Write a response to the novel in any format you choose. What do you like or dislike about the book? Does it remind you of other books or inspire you in different ways? How does the author engage you to read on?

Due: April 5

▶▶   ▶▶   ▶▶

From: Arthur Bean (arthuraaronbean@gmail.com)
To: Kennedy Laurel (imsocutekl@hotmail.com)
Sent: March 23, 10:19

Dear Kennedy,

I would really like to hang out with you this weekend! I never get to see you anymore except at school. Also, I'm going to Edmonton for spring break this week, so I won't get to see you for a whole week! I know that we will have a ton of fun together. I promise! We can do anything you want to do. But let's do something, just you and me, OK?

Yours truly,
Arthur Bean

From: Kennedy Laurel (imsocutekl@hotmail.com)
To: Arthur Bean (arthuraaronbean@gmail.com)
Sent: March 23, 15:53

Hi Arthur!

I know I haven't seen you in a long time! But I feel weird about hanging out just us. I feel a lot of pressure from you to be something I'm not! I hope that doesn't make you feel bad! I still think you're awesome!

Kennedy ☺

▶▶　　▶▶　　▶▶

March 23rd

Dear RJ,

I don't understand. I barely see Kennedy and she says she feels pressure from me?! I called Luke and read him her email, and he said that she's just being a girl and that I shouldn't worry about it and that she probably still likes me. I tried asking Robbie too, but he told me that he doesn't ever want to talk about Kennedy and me.

I just keep asking myself: What would the best boyfriend in the world do in this situation? I wish I knew.

Even *not* dating Kennedy is hard! She's so complicated!

Yours truly,
Arthur Bean

▸▸   ▸▸   ▸▸

From: Von Ipo (thenexteastwood@hotmail.com)
To: Arthur Bean (arthuraaronbean@gmail.com)
Sent: March 24, 14:56

Hey, Artie!

I was talking to a bunch of guys and they said that they would be in our movie as a favor to me! They would make an awesome GGA! Most of them are on my hockey team and they said that their girlfriends would be in the movie too, although a couple of them said that they didn't trust their girlfriends to hang out with just me because they would get dumped! HA-HA! Too funny!

I can rehearse scenes with the guys while you and Robbie are gone this week. Then after spring break we can all get together and do the rest!

Cheers!
Von

▸▸   ▸▸   ▸▸

March 24th

Dear RJ,

I'm so glad that spring break is here. I couldn't handle school anymore. All my teachers hate me, and they gave us so much to do over the break! Ms. Whitehead assigned an entire novel in one week. On our vacation!

Plus, Robbie was in a really bad mood all week, and then Ms. Whitehead called him out in front of everyone for not doing his homework, and he got sent to the office for mouthing off. I tried talking to him about it, but he told me to go bother another one of my loser friends. So I left him alone. Whatever. I don't need him to be my friend if he doesn't want. I'm going to Edmonton, and Luke and I are going to hang out all week, and it will be awesome. Plus, I bet that Dad will have forgotten about the camera by the time I get home. I really hope so!

I won't miss anyone in Calgary while I'm gone. I won't even think about them. Except Kennedy, of course. I'm going to send her a postcard from West Edmonton Mall. Maybe I'll send her two or three! Absence makes the heart grow fonder, so by the time this week is over, she'll be obsessed with me!

Yours truly,
Arthur Bean

▸▸   ▸▸   ▸▸

From: Arthur Bean (arthuraaronbean@gmail.com)
To: Kennedy Laurel (imsocutekl@hotmail.com)
Sent: March 26, 12:31

Dear Kennedy,

I'm in Edmonton right now, and I was thinking about you and wanted to tell you how much I miss you! I was at West Ed today and the whole time I was thinking about how much you would love it here!

When I get my driver's license (I know! That might be planning too far in the future!) we can come up here together. We can go into all the stores and go to the waterslides and stuff. I hope you're having a really great spring break!

Yours truly,
Arthur Bean

From: Von Ipo (thenexteastwood@hotmail.com)
To: Arthur Bean (arthuraaronbean@gmail.com)
Sent: March 26, 16:01

Hey, Artie!

I hope you're having an awesome time in Edmonton. I made the opening credits for *Zombie School*. They look really professional. I took a bunch of Robbie's illustrations and added words and stuff. You'll love them! I'm going to start filming stuff tomorrow with my guys. There's supposed to be a huge snowstorm tonight so we can get some good shots of the outside scenes.

Say hi to your cousin for me! I can't wait to meet him one day. The way you talk about him he's practically famous HA-HA!

Von

▶▶   ▶▶   ▶▶

From: Arthur Bean (arthuraaronbean@gmail.com)
To: Kennedy Laurel (imsocutekl@hotmail.com)
Sent: March 28, 17:17

Dear Kennedy,

I hope you're having a great spring break! I just wanted to tell you that I was in a bookstore today and I saw Kenneth Oppel! He was doing a reading, and I know you love his Frankenstein books. I wanted to get a book for you and get it signed, but the line was really long and I had forgotten my wallet, but I thought about you. I'm not telling you to make you jealous. I just thought, "Man! If only Kennedy were here with me!"

Yours truly,
Arthur Bean

▶▶   ▶▶   ▶▶

From: Arthur Bean (arthuraaronbean@gmail.com)
To: Kennedy Laurel (imsocutekl@hotmail.com)
Sent: March 30, 20:36

Dear Kennedy,

I just wanted to let you know I got home OK, and my spring break was awesome! Luke and I did so much stuff. I took the Greyhound by myself and had both seats to myself on the way home.

Good thing too, because I barely got any work done on Ms. Whitehead's novel assignment while I was away! So I read most of the way home. Did you finish yours? Luke and I were too busy planning the fight scenes for my movie. You're still going to be in it, right? I can write in an awesome part for you, or we can work on it together! You're so great at writing, and if you're involved, your lines will sound more natural than if I write them.

Let me know, and we can work on it after school or at lunch or something.

Yours truly,
Arthur Bean

From: Kennedy Laurel (imsocutekl@hotmail.com)
To: Arthur Bean (arthuraaronbean@gmail.com)
Sent: March 31, 19:40

Hi Arthur,

I'm glad you had a good break. I did a lot of homework, so my spring break has been pretty boring!

Can we talk this week? I think we really need to talk face-to-face!

Kennedy

▸▸   ▸▸   ▸▸

March 31st

Dear RJ,

I just got back home and read Kennedy's email. I tried calling her, but she didn't answer. I can't tell what she's thinking! It kind of sounds serious, so at first I thought that maybe someone had died in her family. If they did, I already have a suit for the funeral. But then I read it again, and I think that maybe she wants to get together. It could be that she missed me over the week and now wants to kiss me again. I'm resolved though, RJ. I will only kiss her if she's my girlfriend. I don't want to be that guy who kisses girls who aren't his girlfriend.

Stay tuned, RJ. I'll let you know!

Yours truly,
Arthur Bean

APRIL

April 1st

Dear RJ,

Something has gone terribly, terribly wrong and I don't know what to do! I was waiting to buy my lunch, and there were two girls in line behind me talking about Robbie. So I started listening to them. They were saying they heard that Robbie stole a video camera this summer and that he was going around stealing kids' phones from their lockers and stuff! I don't know how they heard about the camera, because I never told anyone about it. But they knew about it! Do they think I was involved? I didn't know what to do. I was just glad that I had a newspaper meeting today at lunch so I could get out of there!

I really want to know who told these girls about the video camera. We're supposed to have a movie meeting this week too. How much do people know?! I've been worried about it all day. I don't want to tell Robbie though. He gets so mad about people talking behind other people's backs that he'd probably beat someone up.

And I just realized that I never talked to Kennedy!

Maybe she'll be able to help me, now that we're maybe together.

Yours truly,
Arthur Bean

▸▸   ▸▸   ▸▸

April 3rd

Dear RJ,

I found out who started the rumors about Robbie! It was Catie! I knew I couldn't trust her. Apparently Robbie told her over spring break about taking the video camera, because he's dumb and he tells the wrong people everything, but he swore her to secrecy. And then Catie told everyone that Robbie and his brother are both thieves! I'm so mad at Robbie for telling her about the video camera, but I don't think he knows that everyone else knows. I don't know how to tell him either. Maybe no one will believe it when they find out Catie started it. I sure wouldn't!

But I did avoid Robbie all day today. I didn't want anyone to think I was involved. Is that wrong? I feel bad about it, but I don't want people to think I'm an accomplice! I wonder if everyone now thinks that's why we're making the zombie movie. We should probably deflect attention from that. I wonder if that's why no one came to our auditions. They didn't want to be guilty by association!

Yours truly,
Arthur Bean

⏩   ⏩   ⏩

From: Von Ipo (thenexteastwood@hotmail.com)
To: Arthur Bean (arthuraaronbean@gmail.com)
Sent: April 4, 18:03

Hey, Artie!

Where were you guys today?

I went to our meeting and Ireland said you had canceled! I got a lecture on respecting teachers' time! I told her that you guys had an important reason for not being there, so I think you're in the clear now, buddy!

I wish I'd known beforehand though. My mom was picking me up after our meeting, so I had to just hang around the school for an extra hour till she got there! I showed Ireland what I did over spring break. She was super impressed with how I put everything together! She said that it looked like it was done by a professional.

Anyway, let me know if you want to hang out this weekend to film some scenes. I could probably get the guys together again. They basically look to me to be their social director.

I should get a job on a cruise ship, planning stuff, right? HA-HA!

Von

▸▸   ▸▸   ▸▸

From: Arthur Bean (arthuraaronbean@gmail.com)
To: Kennedy Laurel (imsocutekl@hotmail.com)
Sent: April 6, 10:33

Dear Kennedy,

I'm really sorry I didn't get a chance to talk to you at school this week. I was really busy! My movie is going into production, so we had a lot to do with that. But if you want to hang out this weekend, I can make time for you!

    We can talk face-to-face, just like you want to. Just let me know what time!

Yours truly,
Arthur Bean

▸▸   ▸▸   ▸▸

Dear Ms. Whitehead,

Sorry this assignment is a bit late. I was away for spring break and really busy. But here it is!

Yours truly,
Arthur Bean

Assignment: Personal Novel Study: *Noggin* by John Corey Whaley

by Arthur Bean

Travis Coates is this sixteen-year-old kid who is dying of cancer, but instead of actually dying, he gets his doctors to cryogenically freeze his head. Five years later, they successfully perform a full head transplant, so Travis wakes up with a whole new and healthy and awesome body.

So here are the top five things that I would have done if I were Travis:

1. I wouldn't have been so caught up with my ex-girlfriend. Get over her already!
2. I wouldn't have worn scarves as often. Scars are awesome! But if I was going to wear scarves, I would knit my own awesome ones.
3. I would have tripped more. There's no way he was able to just move around normally in someone else's body.
4. I would have stolen a bunch of stuff because I have new fingerprints and would be able to claim that I didn't know what was happening.
5. I would never have sung a karaoke song in public.

Here are the top five things that I would have done if I were the author of *Noggin*:

1. I would have come to Terry Fox Junior High to talk about my book so that more kids would read it and I could be more famous.

2. I would have written more about the whole head transplant thing and less about the girlfriend thing.
3. I would have mentioned my other books so that kids would know that I wrote more than one book.
4. I would have sworn more, even though there was a lot of swearing already. It sounds more natural.
5. My book would have featured ghosts with no bodies.

Arthur,

This is an original format for your review but doesn't allow for a deep consideration of what you've read. Your thoughtful reflections, as seen in other assignments, are missing in this one. I can't even tell if you enjoyed this book or would recommend it. Next time, dig deeper, please.

Ms. Whitehead

▶▶   ▶▶   ▶▶

From: Arthur Bean (arthuraaronbean@gmail.com)
To: Kennedy Laurel (imsocutekl@hotmail.com)
Sent: April 13, 11:05

Dear Kennedy,

I wish we'd gotten to talk this week. Things were just

so crazy, right? Plus, you must be getting ready for the science fair. I can't wait to see your project.

I don't know if you're around for Easter, but maybe we could talk, like you wanted, sometime this weekend. I'm not really doing anything, and I want to get out of my apartment because Pickles has been eating something that she keeps finding under the couch and then she throws up everywhere, and it's disgusting.

Anyway, we can do whatever you want! There're some awesome movies playing, so we could see one of those, or we could go to Heritage Park again, because that was an amazing time!

Let me know!

Yours truly,
Arthur Bean

▶▶   ▶▶   ▶▶

April 14th

Dear RJ,

Happy Easter, I guess. We didn't do an egg hunt this year, although Dad did ask me if I wanted to do one, and I said no. He seemed a bit disappointed, but he'll get over it. I mean, just because that was the one thing that he used to do when I was a kid doesn't mean that he's the best dad in the world one day a year.

He sure doesn't seem to care about me! I've been home all weekend. I tried to drop hints to my dad that I wanted him to ask why I wasn't hanging out with any of my friends, but he didn't ever ask. The only thing he asks about is the stupid camera. I swear that it's all he cares about. I wanted to shout at him that it wasn't mine or the school's and that Robbie made a mistake and I was paying for it. But I didn't say anything.

Mom would have known right away that something was wrong, and then she would have solved it for me and I could be friends with Robbie and be Kennedy's boyfriend. In fact, she probably would have gotten them to be friends too.

But not Dad. Nope. He's just hanging out in front of the TV.

Yours truly,
Arthur Bean

▶▶   ▶▶   ▶▶

Hey, Artie!

The school science fair is coming up. Would you be able to write something for that? The coverage should be pretty straightforward, and I know you'll use your best objective voice in this article. It's not rocket science... Well, it might be!

Cheers!
Mr. E

▶▶   ▶▶   ▶▶

April 16th

Dear RJ,

Today was even worse than last week. Kids were openly mocking Robbie. They wouldn't leave him alone. Catie's rumor about the video camera has spread, and even some ninth graders heard about his brother being arrested. It was awful to watch. Every time he walked down the hallway, people would say stuff about stealing being a crime, and someone even put a poster of a wanted sign on Robbie's locker. I ripped it off before anyone else saw it when I went to the bathroom during French, but still, it was terrible.

At first I thought Robbie was going to punch someone out, but then he looked like he was going to cry and these ninth-grade boys started making fun of him for crying. That made him super mad, so he was swearing at them and Mr. Everett caught him and sent him to the office.

He wasn't on the bus after school either. I heard he got expelled. I tried calling him, but he won't answer his phone. I don't know what to do. I told Catie to take it all back, but she won't because she says it's the truth.

Why are people so mean?

Yours truly,
Arthur Bean

▶▶   ▶▶   ▶▶

Robbie, what's up? Is everything OK? I heard that you got expelled. Is that true? You weren't at school this afternoon, so I thought maybe it's true! What did you tell Mrs. Winter?

Robbie, stop ignoring me.

Seriously. Stop it.

▶▶   ▶▶   ▶▶

Why weren't you at school today?

You missed a quiz in math! Lucky guy!

Don't make me come over there!

Just kidding!

(Not kidding anymore.)

> You know I will find out what
> happened whether you tell me or
> not. So have it your way. But you
> have to call me about the movie.
> I'm not doing it without you.

▶▶   ▶▶   ▶▶

Science Fair + Carbon Pressing = Mind Blown

by Arthur Bean

This year's science fair at Terry Fox Junior High was held on April 18 in the school gym. There were over a hundred entries this year, a record-breaking number of projects in the science fair, all vying for the top spots to head to the citywide fair in May. Many projects were really awesome, including Kennedy Laurel's piece on fast food and calories, but the competition was fierce and only three groups could nab a coveted spot. The winners of the day included Sandeep Deol and Var Lodhia's Vegetable Clones and Genetic Diversity, Elijah Courzain's project on creating comic book apps, and Jena Frye and Polly VanDusen's Cell Phones and Radiation project. All of those were great, and we hope they do well in the citywide program.

But for this reporter, the coolest thing at the science fair was Jeffrey Wong's project on carbon. More specifically, the coolest part was when he talked about turning people into diamonds. Picture this: Your mom dies and her body is cremated. But you miss her a lot. Instead of having her remains scattered or whatever, you can take her ashes and make them into a diamond. Since our human bodies are made out of carbon (something I learned through Jeffrey's project), that carbon can be compressed into the hardness of a diamond through science!

If that isn't the coolest and creepiest thing you've ever heard, I don't know what is!

Whether you like science or not, the science fair can teach you something.

Hey, Artie,

Not bad, not bad at all! There are a few things that I'd like you to expand upon, and a few cuts to be made (I'm not sure why you've included Kennedy and Catie's project; it's an unnecessary addition), but overall, you've achieved a great tone here.

Cheers!
Mr. E

▶▶   ▶▶   ▶▶

April 22nd

Dear RJ,

Robbie was back at school today! I asked him what happened and he said nothing. So I don't know if he got suspended or what! But it sure doesn't look good for the movie. I asked him about the next production meeting, and he said that he couldn't go because he was grounded. I tried to find out if it was about the video camera and what happened with it, but he just snapped at me and said, "It's not all about you and your stupid little projects. You're not going to get in trouble, dude. So leave me alone." So I left him alone.

I just hope we get to make our movie somehow. But we can't use the camera with people around, and everyone at school hates Robbie. I heard a bunch of kids calling him the Fat Robber. I think some even said it while he was right there. "Don't let the Fat Robber stand behind you at lunch. He might steal your wallet AND your pizza." Robbie isn't even fat! I really don't know what to do, RJ. I guess I was kind of glad that Robbie was a jerk to me and told me to leave him alone. I don't want kids to pick on me either. I had enough of that in elementary school.

Yours truly,
Arthur Bean

▶▶   ▶▶   ▶▶

Assignment: Dilemmas and Cliffhangers

Write a short scene that ends with your protagonist facing a dilemma or being in the middle of a precarious situation.

Remember to choose your vocabulary wisely to portray the gravity of the situation. Find ways to boost the dramatic tension.

Due: May 3

▶▶ ▶▶ ▶▶

April 23rd

Dear RJ,

I didn't think life could get worse, but it has.

I was hanging out with Robbie at lunch today (but in the library, so that no one would bug us) and Kennedy came over. I hoped that she was going to apologize to Robbie for Catie starting rumors, but she definitely wasn't. She said that we needed to talk, so we went outside and she said that she didn't like that I was hanging out with Robbie. She said that I had to stop hanging out with him or else people were going to start thinking I'm a thief too.

I told her that he wasn't a thief and that people were seriously overexaggerating the story, but she said that I had to choose: I can either hang out with Robbie, or I can hang out with her.

How did it come to this?!? I don't want to choose! Robbie's my friend, but I love Kennedy. Plus, she's my almost-girlfriend. It's not fair! I don't understand why Kennedy would even say something like that. She's cooler than that, and I never thought she cared so much about what people think. It's all Catie's fault.

I wonder: What would my mom tell me to do? But then I think, if my mom were here, I would never have agreed to steal the camera because she would have killed me herself if she found out.

Yours truly,
Arthur Bean

▸▸   ▸▸   ▸▸

From: Arthur Bean (arthuraaronbean@gmail.com)
To: Kennedy Laurel (imsocutekl@hotmail.com)
Sent: April 24, 20:31

Dear Kennedy,

I've been thinking about it, and I don't want to have to choose between you and Robbie. He's not stealing phones or whatever people are saying about him. And just because his brother is a criminal doesn't mean that he is too. People are making such a big deal about nothing, and Catie started all these dumb rumors that aren't even true!

I'm also wondering, what do you mean by "hang out"? Like a couple? You know that I really like hanging out with you, and I'll pretty much do anything for you, right? Besides, we don't have to hang out with Robbie together. He can be my friend on the side. We would only hang out with your friends, I promise!

Yours truly,
Arthur Bean

From: Kennedy Laurel (imsocutekl@hotmail.com)
To: Arthur Bean (arthuraaronbean@gmail.com)
Sent: April 25, 22:06

Arthur! They aren't rumors that Catie started. Robbie TOLD her that he stole a video camera! So it's not crazy what people are saying! I don't know why you would want to hang out with a loser like that! If you think that Robbie's a good guy, then you clearly have TERRIBLE TASTE in people! I like you a lot, Arthur, but THIS just won't work if you're friends with the wrong crowd!

Kennedy

▸▸   ▸▸   ▸▸

April 25th

Dear RJ,

I can't decide what to do, so I avoided Kennedy and Robbie at school today. Von also tried to set up an AV Club special meeting this week because we missed the last two, but I told Mrs. Ireland I couldn't go. I hate that my movie is suffering because of all the drama of being in love. Avoidance can't work forever though. (Or can it?) We have the newspaper meeting tomorrow, and she'll probably want to know then who I chose.

If I choose her, I wonder if she'll throw her arms around me and kiss me passionately in front of everyone. That would be pretty romantic. Then we would walk out of school holding hands and everyone would look over and think, "Man. That is the best-looking couple ever!"

Yours truly,
Arthur Bean

▸▸ ▸▸ ▸▸

Hey, Artie!

As you know, the Greenest School initiative is starting in May. I'd love to have a special edition of the <u>Marathon</u> focusing on things that teachers and students are doing to help our planet. Would you like to try writing a feature article?

We'll brainstorm some ideas at our next newspaper meeting, so put on your environmentally friendly cap and start thinking!

Cheers!
Mr. E

▶▶   ▶▶   ▶▶

From: Kennedy Laurel (imsocutekl@hotmail.com)
To: Arthur Bean (arthuraaronbean@gmail.com)
Sent: April 26, 17:19

Arthur!

You RAN out right after Newspaper Club! I really wanted
to talk to you! And today I heard that Robbie actually SPIT
in someone else's food so that he could eat it himself!
    That's DISGUSTING!!

Kennedy

From: Arthur Bean (arthuraaronbean@gmail.com)
To: Kennedy Laurel (imsocutekl@hotmail.com)
Sent: April 26, 19:27

Dear Kennedy,

I'm sorry! I know that we have to talk, but I told Mr. Tan
that I would help move sets for the play coming up, and I
needed to go. I need to stay on his good side so that we
can use the drama room for filming our movie!
    But I promise you that Robbie definitely did NOT spit in
someone else's food. I was with him in line and he would
NEVER do that. People are making up stuff all the time,
and none of it is true. I wish you believed me!
    Anyway, I can't call you tonight because my dad is

really, really strict about phone time after supper, but we can maybe talk at school tomorrow.

Yours truly,
Arthur Bean

▶▶   ▶▶   ▶▶

From: Von Ipo (thenexteastwood@hotmail.com)
To: Arthur Bean (arthuraaronbean@gmail.com)
Sent: April 27, 9:55

Hey, Artie!

I have my whole hockey team and they are totally ready to film all the battle scenes tomorrow! You guys are still free, right? I figured that you probably didn't have anything on Sundays, since you don't play any sports. I also convinced Ireland to let us use the gym after school next week to film the big final scene! I basically told her that she was standing in the way of our learning process if she didn't let us do it! Ha-ha! She totally bought it! Anyway, let me know what time you want to meet! We can just assign roles when we're all there. I have some suggestions written down already. I know what all of the team would be best at, so then we can make sure that we have good people! Did you want me to ask some girls to come too? I'm basically friends with all the girls in our grade, so I'm sure I can get some of them to come!

Von

▶▶   ▶▶   ▶▶

> Von thinks he's filming scenes from the movie tomorrow!

> he can do watever he wants. u mite as well go 2. no 1 wants me there anyway.

> Well, I don't think he can actually film scenes from OUR movie without us both there. If you're not going to go, I'm not going either.

> u go. I think im gonna move away anyway so u need a new art director.

▶▶   ▶▶   ▶▶

From: Von Ipo (thenexteastwood@hotmail.com)
To: Arthur Bean (arthuraaronbean@gmail.com)
Sent: April 28, 23:14

Hey, Artie!

We missed you this weekend! I already had my team ready so we started shooting some scenes. They look AWESOME! I can't wait to show you! Seriously, it's definitely my best work ever! You guys will be at the meeting this week, right? We've got to plan the scenes with the girls in them. Do you think we could write in a part for Tuff to have a girlfriend? A hot girlfriend?

Von

▶▶   ▶▶   ▶▶

April 30th

Dear RJ,

Kennedy dumped me. I got dumped, and we never even really dated. Oh, RJ. Just seeing those words written down makes me want to throw up. I miss her so much already.

We met after school, and I told Kennedy that I thought she was being a bit crazy and that I didn't want to choose between her and my best friend. And she said that sometimes life gave you hard choices. So I told her that I couldn't abandon Robbie right now because if I did, he wouldn't have anyone on his side, and he might move away to a horrible place. She said that I was a good friend who made bad choices, and she was sad that she couldn't benefit from my good friendship. I tried not to cry while she was there, but I couldn't help it, RJ. At least it kind of looked like she was going to cry too. I'm making her sound like she was mean about it, but, RJ, I'm sure that this would never have happened if she wasn't friends with Catie.

I think I made the wrong choice, RJ. I miss her so much. I should have tried harder to be her boyfriend! If I had been better, maybe she wouldn't have cared who my friends are!

Yours truly,
Arthur Bean

MAY

ZOMBIE SCHOOL

by Arthur Bean, Robbie Zack, and Von Ipo

May 2 Production Meeting Notes

I think we should cancel the project, since Robbie won't do it anymore. —AB

No way! You and I have got this, man! I've got all kinds of people lined up, and we can use the gym next Friday after school, and I wrote a new scene for Mai to be a zombie girlfriend to Tuff, but then she tries to eat his face when they're making out and he has to kill her! —VI

I believe that you can move forward with the project with or without Robbie. I expect that he may just need some time for his studies and to work through some family issues.

Let's keep working together and make sure that there's space for Robbie should he decide to return. —Mrs. Ireland

▸▸   ▸▸   ▸▸

May 5th

Dear RJ,

I spent the whole weekend reading books and ignoring people, even my dad. I decided to pretend that I don't exist and started a new novel. I read this book by John Green, and it basically told me that there are worse things in the world than getting dumped. Like having your girlfriend die. That's worse, by a lot, and I have some experience of people dying already, so I know he's right. So after this weekend, I'll go to school and fix everything, somehow.

Yours truly,
Arthur Bean

▸▸   ▸▸   ▸▸

Arthur,

I have not yet received your assignment, which was due on May 3. Being late on assignments is becoming a habit that you need to break. I know you can do better, Arthur! I've seen it so many times! Mrs. Ireland has suggested that your film may be

getting in the way of your schoolwork. It's
important to prioritize your commitments
and, in extenuating circumstances, speak to
me early about getting an extension. Please
see me after class to develop a plan for
future assignments being completed on time
and with effort.

Ms. Whitehead

▶▶   ▶▶   ▶▶

May 6th

Dear RJ,

That's it. I'm quitting school and teaching myself
through movies and books and Wikipedia.

I went back to school and Robbie is being treated
like a piece of snot on a table. Everyone avoids him,
and they make fun of him, and they were even spit-
ting on the ground in front of him while we were
waiting to get on the bus to come home. And he's
a total jerk to me! I'm the only person being nice to
him at all, and instead of being appreciative, I get
Jerk Robbie back. I don't get it.

Plus, everywhere I look, Kennedy's there. Even in
the assembly today, I found her right away in the
bleachers without even looking. Then I couldn't stop
looking for her, making sure she was sitting there

still, watching who she was talking to, thinking about how pretty she looked.

It sucks, RJ. It all SUCKS!

Yours truly,
Arthur Bean

▸▸   ▸▸   ▸▸

Assignment: Dilemma Story

by Arthur Bean

Neal was an accountant. He lived by the book. He liked that he wore a tie to work every day. He drove his tan SUV to work, and he worked out on his lunch hour.

One day, he got an email. Neal, being an accountant, loved getting emails, especially if they had spreadsheets attached. Neal's favorite thing in the world was spreadsheets. Neal opened the email only to find that it was from a Nigerian prince! It took a minute for Neal to decipher the poor grammar and spelling, but essentially, the email said this:

I have three million dollars in an offshore account in your name. This money could be yours, Neal, but only if you give me your bank account information, along with all the spreadsheets on your computer. If you don't do this, not only will you not get the three million dollars, but I, the Nigerian prince, will kidnap your wife and make her my princess.

Neal felt his stomach drop. To be rich but lose all his spreadsheets? Or be poor and lose his wife to a better life as a princess? How could he choose?

TO BE CONTINUED...

Arthur,

I know that you, of all my students, could have come up with a much more interesting dilemma for this assignment. Since you're a serious writer, consider these sorts of tasks good practice for writing bigger pieces, like film scripts and novels. I would appreciate it if you put some effort into elevating your work to a superior quality, especially after our conversation on Monday.

Ms. Whitehead

▸▸ ▸▸ ▸▸

May 9th

Dear RJ,

Another stupid birthday.

I thought you weren't supposed to hate your birthday until you were old and in your thirties.

This morning, Dad woke me up super early, so I didn't even get to sleep in. He asked if I wanted to go out for supper and if I wanted anyone to come, like Anila or Robbie, so that shows just how much he's been paying attention.

And he asked about the camera again! He won't let it go. And he brought up arts camp out of the blue, asking if I wanted to go back and if there was anything I needed to do in order to return. It was so uncomfortable!

Now I'm off to school for another crappy day of crappiness, made all the more crappy because your birthday is supposed to be a great day, so even if it's a normal day, it sucks.

Yours truly,
Arthur Bean

▶▶   ▶▶   ▶▶

May 10th

Dear RJ,

I'm going to write a letter to Kennedy and tell her I love her. I've been working on the perfect draft. Here's what I have so far:

Dear Kennedy,

I just wanted to tell you how much I miss you. I think I made a huge mistake! I should have picked you. You're so perfect and so amazing, and I don't want to not be your boyfriend.

241

*I can be better! I can hang out with you whenever
you want. I'll let you always choose the movies we
watch. I'll never argue with you, even when you say
that Star Wars is sexist and dumb. I'll knit you the
most beautiful sweaters ever, and you can always
choose the color and the patterns. I'll bake you cookies every day, and I'll learn how to make chocolate
cherry cheesecake because it's your favorite dessert!
I'll do ANYTHING you want if you'll be my girlfriend.*

I'm sending it today, RJ! Nothing can stop me!

Yours truly,
Arthur Bean

▶▶   ▶▶   ▶▶

dude do u think that we need a zombie bazooka in the movie?

like instead of shooting bullets it shoots severred heads and then the zombies eat the brains and we go in and kill them while there eating?

Best idea ever! My dad's work just did a big renovation, so they might have some of those giant rolls that carpet comes on. I bet he could get us one if I ask him for it!

> Does this mean you'll be at the next meeting?!

> lets use the stupid camera if its gonna ruin my life anyway, but I can't film till l8r cause my mom's in town and were talking about "our family future." PUKE.

> We can do it later. No problem! You have to tell Von though!

⏩　⏩　⏩

May 10th

Dear RJ,

Never mind. I'll tell Kennedy how I feel later. I got kind of caught up in something else.

Yours truly,
Arthur Bean

⏩　⏩　⏩

May 12th

Dear RJ,

Today Nicole showed up in the morning and said that she wanted to take me to the zoo. I told her that I didn't feel like going to the zoo, but she said that she wanted to see the white tiger they have right now, and she didn't want to go alone and Dan is out of town.

So we went to the zoo. It was the first time I'd been there since I was, like, nine. It turns out she had an ulterior motive. She and Dan are moving in together. They rented a town house in Bowness. I don't know what I was supposed to say. I don't want her to leave, because I'll probably never see her again once she moves. She said she would visit and that we would come for dinner there too, but I doubt it.

But on our way for pizza in Inglewood after the zoo, we were walking along the river, and guess who I ran into.

Anila.

She was there picking up garbage from the riverside with her environment group. And I remembered that I said that I was going to help her do that back in October, and I felt really, really terrible. And then when she said hello and asked how I was doing, all polite and crisp like she always was, I felt so awful about everything that I started kind of crying. RJ, it was so embarrassing! I tried coughing a lot and then I said that I was OK, but that I had really bad allergies, but I think she knew I was lying. So she asked if I wanted to help out with the riverbed cleanup.

Nicole said that she was going to get wool and I could call her when I was done. So I stayed, even though my sneakers got super soaked and my hands were freezing and so gross after.

But I talked to Anila. It was kind of nice, because I could focus on finding cigarette butts or whatever, so I didn't have to look at her. I ended up telling her everything. And, RJ, I mean EVERYTHING. I told her all about taking the camera, and Kennedy making me choose, and about the kids at school being horrible to Robbie, and Robbie's mom coming back and ruining our lives. She just listened. She didn't even seem that mad about anything. She was pretty upset about the camera—after all, her parents are friends with the camp owners—but when I told her that we wanted to return it, she said that she would think about how we could get it back. It didn't sound like she was going to tell the cops about it, so that's a good sign.

She said that she kind of understood how Robbie must feel because she was bullied so badly at her old school that she switched to the one she's in now. I really wanted to ask her what they bullied her about, because I don't know what it could be. Maybe her teeth? Or because she sometimes sounds like she's faking an Australian accent when she talks?

Anyway, I feel kind of OK, except I'm really tired and I just want to sleep. It must be all that garbage picking!

Yours truly,
Arthur Bean

▶▶   ▶▶   ▶▶

ZOMBIE SCHOOL

by Arthur Bean, Robbie Zack, and Von Ipo

May 16 Production Meeting Notes

So stoked that we can film the big final scene next Friday! I talked to everyone about the date change and I've got basically my whole hockey team coming and some of their girlfriends, and I even convinced some of their parents to come and be zombie teachers for us! It's going to be amazing! —VI

how are we going to attach a shovel and bazooka to my arm and make it look real? —rz

You better have not told anyone that they are getting paid, Von! This is strictly volunteer because they want to be famous. I kind of doubt that that many people will be here just for fun. —AB

It would be wise to review the AV Club policy in its entirety before you film, as there are many clauses to the policy that may affect your movie.

Also, please ensure that I have permission forms back from your parents saying that you may stay past 6:00 p.m. on May 24. If I don't have those signed forms, you will not be allowed to continue, for liability reasons. —Mrs. Ireland

▶▶   ▶▶   ▶▶

AV CLUB GUIDELINES—Amended #6

1. Any student may join the AV Club.
2. All equipment must be reserved ahead of time and signed out upon use and signed in upon return.
3. Have fun!
4. Filming must take place in sanctioned school areas. There is no filming in areas restricted to students, such as the basement, the roof, and the staff room.
5. There will be no guns in the film, and other weaponry will be kept to a bare minimum.
6. All equipment must be provided by the students or the drama department. Any additional equipment must be requisitioned through the AV Club administrators.
7. Special effects involving explosions are expressly forbidden.
8. Scripts are necessary to facilitate a successful project.
9. Language in the script and on set must be appropriate for all ages.
10. Parent/Guardian permission must be secured for any after-hours filming.

▶▶ ▶▶ ▶▶

May 19th

Dear RJ,

I've been thinking a lot about stuff this weekend and about losing people. I always thought that it sounded stupid that when someone dies, they say you lost someone. That's not true at all. They're not lost. They're gone.

Like my mom. I didn't lose her. I know exactly where she is. I don't like it, but I know.

So I think that we should change things so that when you break up with someone, you lose them. Because I definitely lost Anila, but then I found her again. I mean, not in the same way, but I think she's still my friend.

I lost Kennedy, but I'll find her again too. After all, we're meant to be together. Even she knows that. She's just too scared to start the rest of her life already.

I think I'm going to lose other people too this year, RJ. I guess it's not just girlfriends but friends too.

Nicole is going to be so far away next year, and with my luck, our new neighbors will be old people who smell like cauliflower and yell about keeping the TV volume down.

I might lose Robbie too if he actually leaves to live with his mom. I wouldn't blame him for leaving. No one at school talks to him except to say crappy things. So then, who will be left?

Yours truly,
Arthur Bean

▶▶   ▶▶   ▶▶

From: Anila Bhati (anila.i.bhati@gmail.com)
To: Arthur Bean (arthuraaronbean@gmail.com)
Sent: May 21, 18:37

Dear Arthur,

I think I've found a way to get the camera back to the camp without anyone noticing. I'm not sure yet, but I'll let you know when I have more details. It might be a bit tricky, but I feel like you're pretty good at sneaking around.

Sincerely,
Anila

From: Arthur Bean (arthuraaronbean@gmail.com)
To: Anila Bhati (anila.i.bhati@gmail.com)
Sent: May 21, 19:02

Dear Anila,

Really? That would be really amazing. I can't wait to hear your plan! And I can definitely be stealthy.

Thanks so much for helping me. I know you don't have to, and I know I was a little bit of a jerk to you, but I'm glad you're such a nice person.

Yours truly,
Arthur Bean

▸▸   ▸▸   ▸▸

> Anila has a plan to get the camera back without ever getting caught!

wat is it?

> I don't actually know yet. But she's really smart, so I trust her. I can't believe she's helping us. Do you think it's because she's still in love with me?

nope, I do not.

> I just hope she doesn't think I'm leading her on. But still, I won't say anything until after the camera is back. We need her on our side!

▶▶   ▶▶   ▶▶

From: Anila Bhati (anila.i.bhati@gmail.com)
To: Arthur Bean (arthuraaronbean@gmail.com)
Sent: May 22, 19:03

Dear Arthur,

OK, I've worked it out.

My parents were invited out to Tomasz and Halina's place for supper on Friday night. I begged my mom to let you and me come. I told her that we had been talking and that we really missed camp and wanted to help get it ready before the summer started. So she asked Tomasz if they needed anything done, and he said that there was definitely stuff we could help with.

So I'll bring my backpack and say it's homework (but it will be the camera).

Then after dinner, we can ask to go look around camp. They'll be talking and won't care, so we can go and hide the camera somewhere where they didn't think of looking for it!

What do you think?

It's pretty simple, but I think it will work. We may have

to do some cleaning while we're there though. I don't really know what kinds of stuff they need us to do.

Sincerely,
Anila

▶▶   ▶▶   ▶▶

> Got your email. Good plan, Anila! But is there any way that you can get them to move dinner to Saturday or Sunday night? We kind of need the camera on Friday.

> Arthur, you can't be serious.

> No, of course not. I'm totally joking! I bet you missed my rapier wit! I asked my dad if I could go, and he said yes. Can your parents pick me up on your way?

▶▶   ▶▶   ▶▶

May 23rd

Dear RJ,

I hope Anila's plan is going to work.

I told Robbie about it and he said that he just wants the camera gone and he doesn't care how we get it back there.

He also thinks no one will show up tomorrow night to shoot the final scene in the gym anyway, so we can film my part later and put the two together using the computer. Robbie thinks Von knows how to do that.

Von acted like he was really upset about me not being there. I can't stand that guy! As if he's not totally happy that he gets to be the star (in his mind) and can steal all my good scenes and awesome lines!

But I'm not thinking about it, RJ. I'm FINALLY going to be able to return the camera and pretend like nothing ever happened. It's even better, because Tomasz will never suspect Anila or me of being involved in actually stealing it. We're just not those people!

Yours truly,
Arthur Bean

▶▶   ▶▶   ▶▶

MISSION ACCOMPLISHED.

wat mission? wat r u talking bout?

The shutter is closed!

> r u texting the rite person rite now? im so lost

> Forget it. I returned the camera.

> oh. cool. thanx

▸▸   ▸▸   ▸▸

May 25th

Dear RJ,

The camera is back! But what a return!

I wasn't sure how we were going to put the camera back, so I made sure that I wore all black to the Zlotys' house. I had a black turtleneck and black pants, and I even wore a black hat. But then, when Tomasz saw me, he asked if I was auditioning for a role as a cat burglar. I was sure he saw my face turn red, but I covered it up by laughing really loud and telling him I was trying out a new look as a slam poet. He thought that was really funny, so then I was off the hook, but Anila looked mortified and made me take the hat off.

I had never actually been in the Zlotys' house before. At camp, it was always kind of off-limits. Not technically off-limits, but there was just no reason to go there. It must be so weird to live at the camp all year long. I wonder if they get freaked out sometimes being so alone in the woods. I would! Their house didn't look scary though. It looked like they took a city house and put it in the woods.

Anyway, just like Anila said, the adults got into some intense and boring conversation, so she asked if there was anything we could do around camp. Tomasz said that he needed all the chairs pulled out from the storage room and wiped down and put at the tables. We almost forgot to bring the camera when we left, so I had to sneak back into the front hall closet and grab Anila's bag. I was so stealthy though. I left my shoes outside the house and slid in on my socks and grabbed the bag really slowly. Then I snuck back out.

It was kind of spooky to be at the camp with no one around. We went into the mess hall, and that's when I had the brilliant idea of hiding the camera underneath the pile of broken chairs and tables at the back of the storage room! We had to drag every single chair (there were like two hundred of them!) out to the tables first, but then at very back, I put the camera under a musty blanket and we left it there. Then we took buckets and sponges and we wiped all the chairs and tables clean.

It was so much work, and I'd forgotten how much Anila talks. She can talk forever! When all the adults came down to tell us that it was time to go, Anila was amazing because she said, "Oh! Tomasz! I think I saw some old electronics in with the broken stuff. Would you mind if I borrowed an old typewriter if you have one?" So then we all went into the storage room, and...there was the camera! Tomasz was so happy. I told him that I actually had kind of spotted it too, but I'd forgotten to say something, so that he didn't think that I was hiding information. Halina said that they had been looking for that camera everywhere, so I said that I remembered a bunch of kids were making a movie about monsters in a closet and so they must have forgotten it in here. I totally covered it up. It was some of the best acting of my life, RJ.

So now the camera is back and no one will ever know that Robbie had it. Maybe there will be other kids from school at camp this year, and they'll think that Robbie never stole it because it will be at camp, and everything will be back to normal next year. That would be awesome. And Kennedy will realize she was wrong, and she'll do anything to make it up to me...and maybe Catie and Von will switch schools. Then everything could be almost perfect.

Yours truly,
Arthur Bean

▶▶   ▶▶   ▶▶

Assignment: Inspired by Emotion

For our major assignment of the year, please take something from your own life over the past year and turn it into a creative writing piece. This can take any form you wish and may be fictionalized, but it must be based on something that happened to you and which evoked a strong emotional reaction.

Remember to incorporate elements of storytelling that we've studied this year into your piece, but the main focus should be on the emotional quotient. Make your reader feel something!

Due: June 14

▶▶   ▶▶   ▶▶

Going Green with Arthur Bean

by Arthur Bean

This is the first of our feature series, "Going Green with Arthur Bean," where I'll be teaching you about new and exciting ways that you can help to save the planet. I've interviewed experts such Anila Bhati, who is the president of the Environment Club at Sam Livingston Academy and a renowned teen environmental activist in Calgary. I've done my research on the Internet too.

I bet you think you're already saving the planet. Sure, you recycle and maybe you even remember a reusable bag sometimes. But I'm here to tell you that that's not enough! You're not doing as much as you can, and because of that, you are killing the earth. That's right. It may be gone before you have grandchildren, and it will be all your fault. So change your ways now, before it's too late!

Everyone has to start somewhere, so I asked teen expert Anila Bhati what her top things would be, and she said that the best thing we can do is pay attention to the food we eat. So here are three tips for you:

1. Go grocery shopping with your mom and tell her to buy

local food more often and eat seasonally. Strawberries don't even taste good in the winter, so you should only buy them when they are around in the summer. Anila says that you'll find that not only are you helping the planet, but you're also helping your taste buds. Food just tastes better when it isn't sitting in a storage room or a truck to ripen.

2. Don't eat sharks. I watched a documentary, and sharks are in danger. Humans kill between sixty-three and 273 MILLION sharks a year. I didn't even know there were that many sharks in the world! It's also really easy to not eat sharks, so I bet most of you already are doing this. So keep up the good work! It's better to have a shark eat you than for you to eat a shark.

3. Compost your food scraps. Calgary has a compost program, but it's only in the southwest communities, so we probably won't get one for a while. But you can also get worm composting kits, which would be awesome because then you have pet worms. Composting is tricky because sometimes it smells bad, and you have to pay attention to it so you don't get maggots, but you don't want to kill the planet, so you should get over how gross maggots are and love them the way you love your new pet worms.

I hope these tips have been helpful to you! I'll be back next year with more "Going Green with Arthur Bean"!

Artie,

I wish I could say I'm surprised by your take on this topic, but I know better by now!

Please confirm that your information is solid—that shark statistic can't be right, can it? Let's tone down the feeling of attack (most people don't want to be blamed), and we can

talk in our meeting about the possibility of
making this an ongoing feature next year.

Cheers!
Mr. E

▶▶   ▶▶   ▶▶

ZOMBIE SCHOOL

by Arthur Bean, Robbie Zack, and Von Ipo

Postproduction Meeting Notes

Friday night was awesome! We got so much filmed, and I spent a bunch of time this weekend putting it together. It's basically done! We make such a great production team! —VI

the animations look cool. i like how u did the zombie grizzly. not bad for an amature. —rz

I'm not sure how you could film the ENTIRE movie without me! I was one of the main characters! We had enough plot for a James Cameron–sized movie. I can't believe you took all of it and made it fifteen minutes long. I can't believe I worked on this all year. What a waste of time. And Von certainly shouldn't have the last name to show up on the credits. People are going to think he did all the work when it was really Robbie's and my idea from the beginning. I basically did all the work here. I just couldn't be there for one day and the whole movie is taken out of my hands? —AB

There is a lot of behind-the-scenes work in filmmaking, Arthur. If you prefer the instant gratification of your art, perhaps join the Drama Club next year. I think Von has done a wonderful job with the piece you all worked on together. —Mrs. Ireland

▸▸   ▸▸   ▸▸

May 30th

Dear RJ,

I can't believe that Von made MY movie without me! I hate that guy! And Robbie seems to think it's really good. I doubt it. I don't even want to see it, except that I kind of want to see it so that I know exactly what I hate about it. It was basically my script (well, mine and Robbie's), and he turned it into a kids' movie. I don't know how he could actually animate Robbie's sketches and make them look good. I can't believe Robbie would let him do that. He must be so upset about his parents and Caleb and stuff that he agreed to it without thinking.

Yours truly,
Arthur Bean

JUNE

u stil mad bout the movie?

Yes.

we can make ur verzon if u want.

No. I never want to work on it again.

k. wanna come over? i have an idea 4 a movie.

Yeah? It is about betrayal?

no. its a robot in a warzone who becomes a destroyer of terrorists.

I'll be there in 30.

▶▶　▶▶　▶▶

From: Von Ipo (thenexteastwood@hotmail.com)
To: Arthur Bean (arthuraaronbean@gmail.com)
Sent: June 4, 17:02

Hey, Artie! I talked to Whitehead today and she said that we could use the movie as our final writing project. I guess Ireland basically told her we were geniuses. Awesome, right?

Von

▶▶   ▶▶   ▶▶

June 4th

Dear RJ,

There's no way I'm sharing a grade with Von and using the movie as my final writing project. I can't believe he thinks it's good. I'm going to show Ms. Whitehead that I write so much better on my own and hand in a way better story than that zombie thing.

Yours truly,
Arthur Bean

▶▶   ▶▶   ▶▶

June 7th

Dear RJ,

It's the second anniversary of Mom's death. I thought about going to school, but then I didn't feel like getting up this morning, so I didn't go. Dad didn't go to work either. It was a bit weird, because we just ate breakfast in front of the TV, but since neither of us are home on weekdays, we didn't even know what to watch, so we just watched game shows. Then Dad said that he wanted to go camping for the weekend, which is just plain weird.

I'm not sure I want to go. I was going to hang out with Robbie. I'm supposed to be packing to go to Banff right this second. Dad said that we can go to the hot springs, which actually sounds pretty fun, although he said that we were going to go hiking on Saturday during the day, which sounds significantly less fun. We used to sometimes go to Banff in the winter and go cross-country skiing, because Mom liked to go. We haven't been there in a long time. I hope that the pizza place I like is still open. I guess, when I stop and think about it, Banff for the weekend is way nicer than going to a graveyard. Maybe Dad finally has a good idea.

Yours truly,
Arthur Bean

▶▶   ▶▶   ▶▶

How waz banf?

Not terrible. I think I like camping. I learned how to make a fire and what berries will kill you. I'm on my way to being a mountain man. Now I just need a beard. Ha!

Dude u with a beard is the funiest image ever! Check it out!

▶▶　　▶▶　　▶▶

June 10th

Dear RJ,

My camping trip with Dad was very strange, but in kind of a good way. For one thing, we talked a lot.

It was mostly not about anything important, but he told me stories about camping when he was a kid and that kind of stuff. Turns out my dad loves camping, but my mom hated it, so we never went. One night when we were sitting by the fire (because, RJ, it's so cold in the mountains at night that I wanted to die sometimes), he brought up the video camera again. He was so sneaky about it. He just casually asked if I had returned the camera to camp last week. So I said yes. And he said, "Good. I didn't want to have to return it for you. Don't do that kind of stuff." And I said, "I won't." And he said, "Good."

That was it. I wish I knew how he knew I was lying about it. I wonder why he didn't say anything before. Plus, how would he have returned it without me getting into trouble? I'm glad that he didn't do that. But why wouldn't he have grounded me or said something to make me feel bad? That would have been way easier than sneaking around!

Yours truly,
Arthur Bean

▶▶   ▶▶   ▶▶

Assignment: The Franklina Diamond

by Arthur Bean

Chet and Franklina were the world's best couple from eighth grade until they both became famous writers.

Things were going so great, and Chet couldn't wait to get married. So he proposed one night, at sunset, on a cliff overlooking the ocean next to Hollywood, where they lived.

Franklina was so overwhelmed, she screamed, "Yes, I'll marry you!" But then the giant diamond engagement ring caught the reflection of the sun, and Franklina was momentarily blinded, lost her balance, and toppled over the cliff into the turbulent waters below. By the time Chet got down the cliff and hauled her body out of the water, she was very, very dead.

Chet was devastated. The love of his life was gone forever. He couldn't handle the idea of never seeing her again. He needed to have her with him, otherwise he couldn't exist.

That week, Chet walked the streets of Hollywood in his grief, looking for answers. On the day before the funeral, he walked past a storefront he had never seen before. It was right beside his penthouse apartment, and he was shocked that he had never noticed it before, because it looked like it had been around since before California was settled. In the musty window, there was a sign that read:

Did Your True Love Die?

Keep Them Around Forever. Ask Us How!

Of course, Chet entered.

As soon as he entered, the old woman behind the counter said, "Hello, Chet."

Chet was startled. "How do you know my name?" he asked.

"It's written on your sleeve," she said. Chet had forgotten that he was wearing his high school football jacket. "But I sense your grief. Let me help you."

Chet sat down. "This sadness. It is too much. You need this girl. You need her forever," the woman said.

Chet nodded. He couldn't talk without crying.

"I can help you keep her around, if you want," the woman said.

"Like a zombie?" Chet cried.

"No. But I can make her into a diamond."

Chet looked at her disbelievingly.

The old woman seemed to know what he was thinking. "I will take her body and compress it. I know how to turn human remains into the world's hardest carbon. Then I will put that diamond in a ring that looks like you won the Super Bowl. Then your girlfriend will be with you always. She will always be connected to you."

Chet thought about what she had said. "I am very famous and rich," he said. "But this sounds very expensive. How much will it cost me?"

"Nothing," she chuckled. Then she muttered under her breath, "Yet..." But Chet didn't hear that part. He was too busy thinking about how this was the best way for him to keep Franklina with him every day, forever.

"I'll do it," he said.

The woman chuckled again. "I knew you would. Leave the rest to me. Come back in a week and I will have your Franklina diamond."

The week passed slowly. When he finally got the diamond, it was beautiful. The ring looked just like a Super Bowl ring. And in the right light, Chet was sure the diamond looked exactly like the sparkle in Franklina's eyes. It was perfect. Chet thanked the woman profusely. She just chuckled and said, "I wouldn't thank me, son. Not even a little..." Chet thought this was weird, but he left wearing his Franklina diamond.

He immediately felt lighter. When he walked down the street, he could feel Franklina's hand in his. It really was like she was with him again.

But then, one day, he was walking through a department store and all of a sudden, his hand reached out and grabbed a perfume bottle and tucked it into his coat. He tried to take it out, but his hand wouldn't let him. He ran out of the store carrying the perfume bottle. It smelled familiar... It was the same perfume that Franklina had worn.

The next day, the same thing happened. His hand would reach out and steal stuff, and he was helpless to stop it. It happened again and again. He looked down at his new ring. The twinkle in the diamond looked mischievous, even...evil.

He whispered to the ring, "Stop it. Whatever you're doing, stop it." But then his own hand slapped him hard across the face. The people on the street stopped and stared, so he kept walking.

It got worse. Within a few days, Chet wasn't able to leave his house without his hand stealing things or pushing old ladies over. He was at his wit's end. "Franklina, I know you're angry to be a diamond. But you know I love you! I can't do this anymore!" He tried to take the ring off, but it wouldn't work. Nothing would make the ring come off.

The next day, he went out to find the old woman. But where the shop was before, there now stood an empty lot. There was no sign of the old woman at all. Chet may have imagined it, but he was sure he heard the ring chuckle.

After another terrible day of stealing things and pushing old ladies, Chet sat in his kitchen, holding a butcher knife over his Super Bowl ring. He had tried everything and he knew this was his last option. He brought down the knife...

The next morning, Chet awoke with a dull pain in his left hand. He looked down to where his ring finger used to be. It was only gauze and pain now. He smiled sadly to himself. He had never thought he would want to be rid of Franklina, but maybe he was better alone. He turned over to face the window. As he did, there was an extra sparkle that caught the light. It looked exactly like the refraction of light that had killed his true love.

He looked down, only to see the Franklina diamond on his other hand.

Arthur,

I'm pleased to see that your writing skills have improved over the year. You've done a nice job incorporating different elements of storytelling into your narrative. "The Franklina Diamond" is very engaging; however, it's also extremely dark in content. I'm uncertain how it matches with the final assignment parameters. What emotion and event in your life were you trying to incorporate into this story?

Ms. Whitehead

Ms. Whitehead,

Actually, this story is very close to my life. I've loved and I've lost. Plus, this past weekend, I almost cut off my own finger with an ax. You shouldn't be so quick to assume you know everything about me. I'm very versatile.

Arthur Bean

▸▸   ▸▸   ▸▸

June 17th

Dear RJ,

I saw Kennedy today in the hall, and we actually talked. It was amazing. I think she's realized that she was being too harsh about Robbie. She's way more awesome when Catie's not around. She seemed kind of sad that I'll be at camp all summer, since her family is staying in town for part of July. Maybe I can take a few days and come back to hang out with her.

It's funny, actually. I haven't heard from Anila. I thought she would be calling me all the time again, but she hasn't called once. I called her to thank her for helping me and she was nice and all, but otherwise, nothing. I wonder if she's playing it cool so that I think she's not into me anymore. I hope it's not weird at camp because of our history together!

Yours truly,
Arthur Bean

➤➤   ➤➤   ➤➤

Hey, Artie,

I'm hoping that you're available to come by my classroom at lunch today. I would like to talk to you and Kennedy about an opportunity on the Marathon staff for next year.

Cheers!
Mr. E

➤➤   ➤➤   ➤➤

From: Kennedy Laurel (imsocutekl@hotmail.com)
To: Arthur Bean (arthuraaronbean@gmail.com)
Sent: June 18, 20:40

Hi Arthur!

I wanted to MAKE SURE that you're seriously OK with us being coeditors of the *Marathon* next year! I TOTALLY understand if you decide not to do it because you would have to work with me. Plus, you probably have heard by now that I have a new boyfriend, so I just don't want things to be awkward between us. I already asked Catie if she wants to be our fashion reporter next year. I've got a million great ideas, so I hope you're ready!

ALSO, I watched your little zombie movie! Mrs. Ireland showed it to our class! It was AWESOME! You and Von did SUCH a good job! I could totally see your sense of humor! It was HILARIOUS!

Kennedy ☺

From: Arthur Bean (arthuraaronbean@gmail.com)
To: Kennedy Laurel (imsocutekl@hotmail.com)
Sent: June 18, 21:16

Dear Kennedy,

I'm glad you liked our movie. Von kind of took over and butchered my vision for the film, so I wasn't exactly involved in the final direction the film took. But he showed our English class too, and I guess it did look pretty good in the end. It wasn't supposed to be that funny, but I'm sure that happens all the time. Von and I never had the same artistic vision for the movie anyway. I think I'm more of a live theater kind of guy. Movies are for people who can't handle improvising.

I think the newspaper is going to be great next year. I've already asked Robbie to be our art director, so he and Catie will have to work together a lot. He hasn't said yes, but I'm sure we're all professional enough to get along.

Yours truly,
Arthur Bean

▶▶   ▶▶   ▶▶

June 18th

Dear RJ,

Well, I know the first thing I'm doing as editor of the *Marathon* next year: firing Catie. And like I care that Kennedy has a boyfriend. She never dates anyone for a very long time anyway! I have barely thought about her at all this month.

No word on how Robbie's mom's custody case is going these days. I guess the divorce is final, and Robbie said she's moving to Lethbridge without her boyfriend so that she can be closer to Robbie and Caleb. He said that Caleb is definitely going to move down there, but he doesn't know what he'll do yet. I've got all summer at camp to make sure he doesn't go. Wish me luck!

Yours truly,
Arthur Bean

▶▶   ▶▶   ▶▶

Assignment: The Gratitude Project: Thanks to You

This year's Gratitude Project and other English assignments were meant to bring some reflection on what shapes you. But it's not just outside sources that mean something. Write a short paragraph reminding yourself of all the great work you did this year. It's important that we are kind to others, but also that we are kind to ourselves!

Due: June 20

▶▶   ▶▶   ▶▶

Assignment: Thanks to…You

by Arthur Bean

Dear Arthur,

You're a great guy, but hopefully you know that. You didn't accidentally kill Pickles, and you never on purpose killed Von, even though you often wanted to. You made two girls fall in love with you, and even though you're single now, watch out! The ladies will be after you one day! I think your Franklina Diamond story has some real grit to it, and one day you'll be famous for writing. I bet you write the next Star Wars, but not actually, because someone else is doing that. You're one heckuva guy!

Arthur,

It sounds like you had a roller coaster of
a year, personally and creatively. I hope
that you do continue writing enough to be
famous; you've got the talent, the creative
spirit, and you most certainly have the drive
to succeed. I look forward to seeing what
ninth grade brings for you—hopefully, a
better understanding of deadlines!

Ms. Whitehead

YEAR-END REPORT CARD

Arthur did some fine work this year in class. His sense of humor and unique perspective are evident in his writing, and his sense of story and critical-thinking techniques have developed. Arthur's extracurricular endeavors occasionally got in the way of handing assignments in on time. It's wonderful that his passion for writing is so strong, but it is important that he prioritize work properly.

Ms. Whitehead

Arthur Bean
English 8B—Ms. Whitehead
Year-End Summary

Introduction Paragraph	Complete
Description and Imagery	86%
Using Symbolism	71%
Gratitude Project: Letter to a Veteran	74%
Creating an Effective Setting	84%
Persuasive Writing	78%
Introductions and Thesis Statements	80%–5% = 75%
Gratitude Project: Letter to a Loved One	61%–5% = 56%
Judge a Book by Its Cover	77%
Tweet Your Book Review!	80%
Personal Novel Study	70%–5% = 65%
Dilemmas and Cliffhangers	63%–5% = 58%
Major Assignment: Inspired by Emotion	85%
Gratitude Project: Thanks to...You!	Complete

NOTE that assignments handed in late are subject to a 5% reduction.

ACKNOWLEDGMENTS

Thank you to Sandy Bogart Johnston, Simon Kwan, Aldo Fierro, and Erin Haggett, along with the rest of the amazing, wonderful team at Scholastic; a finer home for Arthur couldn't be found.

Thank you Dorothea Wilson-Scorgie and Bill Radford, as well as the Inkslingers gang: Kallie George, Shannon Ozirny, Tanya Lloyd Kyi, Lori Sherritt-Fleming, and Maryn Quarless, for insightful comments and support. Thanks to Paul Battin for a rainy canoe trip down the Yukon River (you should have brought your coat), and to Jennifer Macleod and Sarah Maitland for the carbon-pressing story ideas over french fries at the Café.

And of course, thank you to my whole family for not only being awesome, but also for being key marketers for my first book, making sure that everyone we've ever known bought at least three copies. (On that note, thanks to everyone we've ever known for buying three copies of Arthur's first adventure.) Robert, Diane, Curtiss, Andrew, Chelsey: we're the best family I've ever met.

ABOUT THE AUTHOR

Stacey Matson's debut, *A Year in the Life of a Complete and Total Genius* began as her master's thesis at the University of British Columbia. It has received many accolades, including being chosen as a Junior Library Guild pick, a CLA Notable Children's Book in the Language Arts, and an Indie Next Pick.

Stacey's non-writing occupations have been intriguingly varied—from running a Christmas tree lot to performing as a fairy princess at birthday parties. Stacey lives in Vancouver. Visit her at staceymatson.com.